CHRISTMAS AT THE STABLES ON MUDDYPUDDLE LANE

Heart-warming, uplifting romance

Etti Summers

CHAPTER ONE

Amos walked slowly down the stairs, gripping the handrail and wincing at the ache in his right knee. It was playing up something rotten this morning, and he reminded himself to add some ibuprofen gel to the shopping list. He'd pop into Picklewick later and pick up a few bits and pieces, and he'd pay a visit to the care home whilst he was there. He liked to call in once or twice a month, knowing that the residents welcomed his visits. Actually, it wasn't so much they wanted to see **him** – they loved seeing Queenie, Petra's black Cocker spaniel.

The dog in question was curled up in her basket next to the fire, he noticed, as he entered the kitchen. Patch, the little Jack Russel terrier that belonged to Nathan, the stable's general manager, was also crammed in with her. Both dogs opened their eyes when they saw him and Queenie wagged her tail, but neither got out of bed and he didn't blame them. It might be seven-thirty in the morning, but it was pitch-black outside and freezing.

Amos pulled a face. He was late on parade again. Petra, Harry and baby Amory were already up and getting on with their day. Lately Amos was finding it hard to get out of bed in the mornings. He might blame it on the time of year, but he had a nagging suspicion that age was creeping up on him. Seventy-three wasn't old, not these days, not when pop icons who were older than him were still touring and actors in their seventies and eighties were still churning out block-buster films, but try telling that to his stiff joints and aching back.

As the day wore on and he moved around more, he would gradually loosen up, but right now he felt like a mechanical metal toy that had rusted up and needed a good dose of oil.

'Morning,' he muttered, smelling the mouth-watering aroma of frying sausages. 'If you'd have waited, I'd have cooked those.'

Harry was at the stove, a wooden spatula in his hand. 'It's okay. We were up, so I thought I'd make a start on breakfast. There's tea in the pot.'

Grumpily, Amos took a seat at the scarred wooden table and Petra smiled at him.

She had little Amory on her lap and the baby's face lit up when he saw his great-great-uncle, and he held out his chubby arms.

Petra passed the baby over. 'He slept through again last night,' she said. 'I think we've cracked it.'

She still looked tired, but not as exhausted as previously. Mind you, Amos wasn't surprised that she was knackered: what with the stables to run, a six-month-old baby, and a new holiday let business to get off the ground, she'd had a busy few months. And she'd even managed to get married in the middle of it.

Harry hadn't been slacking, either. He'd done what he could around the stables whilst continuing to work as a farrier, and he also did his fair share of looking after the baby – which was why Amos felt guilty for sleeping late again. Because of his angina, Petra wouldn't let him do any physical work, so the least he could do was keep his little family fed. The kitchen had become his domain, and although he knew he was being silly, he resented anyone else cooking in it.

'Sausage sandwich?' Harry asked.

Amos wasn't resentful enough to turn down a sausage sandwich. 'Yes, please. Red sauce.'

'That's so wrong,' Harry joked. 'It has to be brown. Everyone knows that. Here you go.' He put a plate in front of him.

'Ta.' Amos picked up half of the sandwich, careful to keep it out of the reach of grabby starfish hands, and took a bite. Not bad, he conceded. If he wasn't careful, he'd be out of a job.

'I'm going into Picklewick this morning,' he said, between mouthfuls of the butcher's finest pork and beef sausages and his own bread, baked fresh this morning. His final task every evening was to fill the bread maker, so the family could wake up to a freshly baked loaf. 'Would you like me to take Amory?'

'It's okay,' Petra said. 'I'm planning on spending today in the office, so he can stay here with me.'

Amos didn't show it, but he felt a little aggrieved. Paperwork was his job, too.

'Oh?' was all he said.

'It's about time I got to grips with the accounts,' she explained. 'It's not fair leaving it all to you.'

'I honestly don't mind doing them,' Amos said, but even as the words left his mouth, he understood Petra's reasoning. He wasn't getting any younger and at some point she'd have to take over. It made sense for her to start now. If he suddenly popped his clogs, she wouldn't know where to begin.

'I know you don't,' she soothed. 'But I expect you've got other things to do today.'

Not much, he thought. Aside from a bit of shopping and cooking the evening meal, he was at a loose end. He supposed he could defrost the freezer, but it was currently full of festive food so it would probably be better to leave it until after

Christmas. He could always clean the oven. However, there was one thing holding him back – it was a job he hated doing and invariably put off for as long as he could.

'I'll finish my breakfast,' he said, 'then I'll see to the chickens.'

They were let out of their coop every morning to roam free during the day, then rounded up again in the evening so the foxes didn't get them. He'd heard one barking last night when he'd woken up to go to the loo, but had then taken ages to get back to sleep. Gone were the days when he'd slept like the dead and woke refreshed in the morning. These days he was more like the walking dead!

Petra made faces at her son, who chortled back at her. 'It's okay, Nathan has already done it. One of the holidaymakers wanted to take a dozen home with them and they are leaving early, so I asked him to pop some down to them before they go.'

'Right.' Amos's voice sounded flat. Considering there was always something that needed doing when there were loads of animals to look after, there seemed to be surprisingly little for him to do. Or should he say, there was little that Petra **allowed** him to do.

Maybe 'allowed' was the wrong word – after all, the stables belonged to him, although it would go to Petra once he was gone – but she fussed over him so much if she thought he was over-exerting himself that it simply wasn't worth the hassle. Anyway, he knew she was right, and he didn't want to risk an angina attack. Gentle pottering was what he had been reduced to these days; and to think that when he was younger he never used to think twice about throwing bales of hay around or wrangling a stroppy horse.

Things had moved on since then, some for the better, such as Petra coming into his life and baby Amory, and others not so good. Top of the not-so-good list was losing his wife to cancer. Whoever had said that time was a great healer was a big liar, because Amos missed Mags as much now as when she'd first passed. More so, because he couldn't help wondering what she would have made of all these changes.

For years he and Petra had been on their own at the stables, apart from Nathan, but when Harry had taken over old Ted's farrier business a couple of years ago, their lives had been turned upside down.

First, Harry had moved into the stables with them, then shortly after he had dreamt up a new business venture in the form of converting an old cow shed into holiday lets, and on top of that, Petra had discovered she was pregnant. Amory had arrived early, bless his little cotton socks, and then she and Harry had got married.

This past year had been all go, so Amos should be thankful that things were now on an even keel and they had a chance to draw breath. Instead though, he felt unsettled and out-of-sorts, and he had no idea why.

Oh, how he wished Mags was still alive.

But if wishes were gold, he'd be a rich man, so there was nothing for it but to get on with it. At least he'd be able to cheer up some old folk this morning.

The irony that he was probably only a few years younger than the residents themselves, wasn't lost on him.

'How is Mum today?' Lena Rees asked as she approached the reception desk in the foyer of Honeymead Care Home and glanced around at the glittering Christmas tree in the corner, decorated in gold, and at the fairy lights draped around the large mirror on the wall next to it. It all looked very festive, as was the smell of berries and cinnamon perfuming the air. But she wasn't in the mood for Christmas. Her mum hadn't been herself lately and Lena was worried.

Charity Jones was manning the desk this morning and she looked up from her computer screen and smiled. 'She's had a good night, I believe, and she's eaten some breakfast. A bit of porridge and some fruit.'

'Grapefruit?' Lena asked, hopefully. Half a grapefruit was her mum's favourite, even though it sometimes gave her heartburn.

'No, just a couple of raisins.' Charity's smile was sympathetic. She was as aware as Lena, that Olive's appetite had decreased steadily since the summer, and Lena felt like crying. Her mum was fading before her very eyes and there was nothing anyone could do about it. Old age, the doctor had said. His smile had been sympathetic, too.

'She's in the day room,' Charity informed her. 'I tried to persuade her to have her nails done because we've got a manicurist in today, but she wasn't keen.'

Her mum wasn't keen on anything these days, Lena thought. 'I'll make her a cup of tea, then go on in,' she said.

'I'll bring it through, if you like?' the girl offered. The care home had a cafe area, where residents and visitors alike could help themselves to hot drinks, cakes and biscuits.

'That's kind of you, but I can manage. You've probably got lots to be going on with.' Lena had a great deal of time for Charity. She was a lovely girl, and was only a few years younger than Lena's own daughter, October. October worked at the stables on Muddypuddle Lane as a groom, and Charity also helped out there in exchange for stabling her horse.

Charity was a favourite of her mother's too, and she and Olive had originally bonded over Charity's tales of the antics the animals at the stables got up to. Plus, Charity brought cat food in for Marmalade.

It had worried Lena to death when her mum had been caught sneaking food out of the dining room. She used to secrete roast potatoes, pieces of fish, and on one occasion even a dollop of trifle, in her pockets. Lena had been convinced that Olive must be suffering from dementia, until Charity discovered that her mum had been feeding a stray cat.

Lena had still been a little concerned about her mum's mental health, because Olive was quite savvy when it came to animals and she should have been aware that cats didn't like trifle. But Lena was wrong. The cat did indeed like trifle. It also liked mashed potato, cheese, cake (but only if it had buttercream icing on it) and blackberries. Lena had stood corrected, and was no longer concerned about the state of her mum's mind. If anything, the old lady was sharper than she was.

Lena was very worried about her mum's physical health though, because the old lady had been growing noticeably frailer over the past few months, and Lena had a horrible feeling that she mightn't be around for much longer.

The thought of being without her mum filled her with dread. Her mother had been such a rock over the years, especially when Lena had discovered she was pregnant all those years ago and the baby's father hadn't been interested. Olive had shored her up, in more ways than one, and had convinced her that she was totally capable of raising a child on her own.

They had always been close and they still were, and Lena simply couldn't imagine life without her mum in it.

But she knew there would come a time when she'd have to do more than imagine, because Olive was ninety-three, and was lately showing less and less interest in things. She seemed to be withdrawing into herself, and not even the excitement of putting the Christmas decorations up had lifted her out of it. She used to love Christmas so much, unlike some of the other residents who did nothing but grumble about the festive season, that it gave Lena even more reason to worry.

When she stuck her head around the day room door, Lena spotted her mum sitting in front of one of the large picture windows – her favourite spot of late – with a black spaniel at her feet. The old lady was bending forward to pet the dog's silky head. It was the most interest she'd shown in anything for weeks and Lena's spirits rose.

Her mum loved animals, and the highlight of her week was when Amos came to visit. Sometimes he brought Petra's baby boy too, so Olive had a double dose of cuteness.

Amos would work his way around all of the residents who wanted to stroke the dog, but he always seemed to spend more time with Olive.

'Hi, Mum, how are you today?' Lena asked, putting the cups of tea down on a side table, and planting a gentle kiss on the wrinkled cheek.

'Not so bad,' her mum said, but Lena could tell she wasn't being entirely truthful.

 Trying not to let her worry show, she turned to Amos. 'Hello, Amos, how are you? I've brought you both some tea,' she lied. She had a soft spot for Amos, and she would happily forgo a cup of tea so that he could have it instead.

'You're a gem,' Amos said to her, taking a sip. He looked tired, not his usual bubbly self, and a ripple of unease travelled down her spine.

'Where's the baby today?' she asked and saw his expression cloud over.

'He's with his mum. She's in the office this morning, so my services aren't required.' He looked crestfallen and she wondered why that should be an issue.

She knew he loved the baby to bits and enjoyed looking after him, but surely this was only for one day? No doubt Petra would be back in the saddle tomorrow. Literally, because she would probably take one of the horses out for some exercise.

Lena's unease continued to linger. She knew all about Amos's angina and she prayed that his heart wasn't giving him any more trouble. She also knew that Petra, Harry, Nathan, and her own daughter, all made sure he didn't exert himself, and she vowed to give October a ring later to ask if she knew what was wrong.

'I'd better do the rounds,' he said, gesturing to an old gent who was staring intently at the dog.

Lena smiled. 'You better had. Brian adores Queenie.' Brian was a lovely old man who suffered with dementia. Prior to moving into the home, he'd had a dog, and Lena knew how badly he missed the animal. But he increasingly forgot that his dog had been rehomed, and when he remembered, the poor chap broke his heart all over again.

Her gaze followed Amos and Queenie, and she saw Brian's face light up as he ruffled the dog's ears.

In contrast, her mum's expression was blank. She was staring out of the window, her eyes distant.

'You love Queenie too, don't you, Mum?' Lena said in a jolly tone.

Her mother twitched a shoulder, which Lena took as a yes.

She bit her lip and tried again. 'What did Amos have to say for himself? Any funny stories about the animals?' Her mum loved hearing about what the horses and the other creatures who lived at the stables got up to.

Olive brought her attention back to Lena with a tangible effort. 'Amos was telling me about Princess.'

'What has that flippin' goat been up to now?' Lena sing-songed. She knew she sounded like an adult talking to a child, but she couldn't seem to help herself.

'She managed to get into the boot room and ate one of Amos's flat caps.'

Ah, that was better: her mum seemed to have perked up a bit.

Lena laughed. 'The little madam! I've never come across such a naughty animal. And she's teaching her kid bad habits too.'

'I want to go outside,' Olive said abruptly.

'Er, okay. If that's what you want, I'll get your coat. You'll need a hat and a scarf, as well. But are you sure? The garden doesn't look its best at this time of year, and it's not very nice out there. In fact, it's freezing. Brrr,' she added, theatrically.

'I don't want to go into the **garden.**'

Lena was confused. 'Where do you want to go?' she asked, before realising what her mum wanted. 'Oh, I see, do you want to go out to lunch?'

Until recently her mother had been able to shuffle around using a walker, but over the past few months her mobility had worsened. It would be difficult to load the wheelchair into the car, and get her mum in and out of the passenger seat, but Lena would manage somehow.

'I don't want to go out to lunch. Or shopping. I want to go **there**.'

When Lena followed her mother's gaze, she sucked in a sharp breath. Olive was staring at the view, which consisted of rolling hills leading up to the moorland. She could just make out the stables from here and Lilac Tree Farm above it.

'You can't!' she cried.

'Why not?' Olive's chin jutted out like a sulky child.

Lena floundered. Where should she begin? 'It's just not possible.'

'Amos could take me.'

'Amos?'

'He lives at the stables, doesn't he? He could drive me. I want to smell fresh air and heather, and I want to feel the wind in my face again before I die.'

'Mum! Don't say that!'

Her mother gave her a keen look. 'It happens to all of us – some sooner than others. I've had a good life and been blessed with a wonderful family, but I'd like to see horses again.'

'I've got some photos on my phone. October shared them with me—'

'That's not what I mean and you know it,' her mum interjected. 'I've not got long left, Lena. I just want to...' She ground to a halt, then waved her hand in the air and sighed. 'Ignore me, I'm just being silly. Tell me, what are you going to do with the rest of your day?'

Lena blinked as the abrupt change of topic caught her by surprise. 'Erm, I don't know.'

'Why don't you go have some fun?' Olive suggested.

'Fun?'

'Yes, you know...do something you enjoy, something that brings you happiness.' When Lena continued to gaze at her with a stricken expression, her mum tutted and rolled her eyes. 'I'm tired,' she said abruptly. 'You get off home. I think I'll have a nap.'

'You've not long got up,' Lena protested. It was only ten-fifteen.

'Yes, well...'

The animation in her mum's face had drained away and Lena felt like crying, because she knew in her heart that her mum was right – she **didn't** have long left.

The thought was unbearable.

'Excuse me,' Amos said to Brian, as he saw Lena hurry out of the day room. She looked upset and he couldn't let her leave without asking if there was anything he could do to help. 'Queenie, come,' he commanded. 'I'll be right back,' he promised the old chap.

Queenie leapt to her feet and followed obediently as Amos hastened after Lena.

He caught up with her just as she was about to step outside. 'Lena!' he called. 'Wait.'

Lena halted but she didn't turn around, and when he reached her, he realised why.

She was crying.

'Whatever is the matter?' he asked.

Lena blinked furiously. 'It's nothing.'

'It is clearly **something,**' Amos said, gently taking hold of her arm. 'Why don't we go over there, where it's nice and quiet and have a cup of tea?'

Lena sniffed and allowed him to lead her to a chair in a quiet corner of the cafe area. He fetched her a cup of tea and one for himself, and sat down opposite. 'Now, then,' he said. 'What's all this about?'

Lena looked up at the ceiling, blinking furiously, her chin wobbling. 'It's Mum. She says she doesn't think she's got long left.'

'Ah.' Amos pulled a face. He had also noticed that Olive had become more distant over the past few months, but he hadn't liked to say anything.

'She's right,' Lena added. 'I've been thinking the same thing myself, but it shocked me when she came right out and said it.'

'I expect it did.'

'The doctor says old age is catching up with her.'

'Is there anything I can do?' he asked, guessing the answer would be no, but offering anyway.

Lena gave him a small sniffling smile as she dabbed a tissue to her cheeks. 'Not unless you can turn back time.'

'If I could do that, I'd have done it already,' he said, his thoughts gravitating towards Mags.

'I suppose you would. I'm sorry, that was thoughtless of me,' Lena said, and Amos immediately felt awful.

'There's nothing to be sorry for,' he hastened to assure her.

'At least my mum has had a good long life,' she said, wiping away her tears and blowing her nose.

'October tells me she used to ride. As did you,' he said, turning the subject away from his wife. Although he usually loved talking about Mags as a general rule, for some reason it didn't feel right discussing her with Lena.

'She did,' Lena said, and Amos was relieved to see that she was no longer crying. 'Mum was a pretty good horsewoman in her day, if I remember rightly,' she added.

'What about you?' Amos had known Lena ever since she had moved to Picklewick about ten years ago to look after Olive. She had helped with clearing the cow shed prior to the builders coming in, and she had been there for him when Petra had gone into early labour. In fact, Lena had insisted on making sure that the nursery was ready for little Amory when the baby was eventually discharged from hospital. She had also helped organise the surprise reception for Petra and Harry's wedding, and she had stepped in to help when the wedding was delayed because of a grass fire.

But he didn't really know her as well as he should, and when the sudden thought that he would like to get to know her much better and in a way that wasn't at all platonic, popped into his head, his eyes widened and his breath caught in his throat.

Fancy him having thoughts like this at his age! After Mags died, he'd assumed that this kind of thing was behind him. Apparently not. Which was daft considering that only this morning he had felt every one of his seventy-three years and then some. He should be past all this nonsense at his age, but here he was fancying a woman nearly ten years younger than him and one who had so much life left to live. She would never give an old codger with a dicky heart a second glance.

'I haven't ridden for years,' Lena was saying. 'I used to love it, but life kind of got in the way.'

'So that's where October gets her love of horses from – you as well as Olive?' He hadn't known Lena could ride, although he knew that Olive used to. It had been a good few years since he'd been on the back of a horse himself.

 Lena smiled. 'It's more than love with October, it's an obsession.'

Amos nodded his understanding. Lena's daughter had worked at some of the best show jumping yards in the country, but she had never quite made it in that highly competitive world. She had come to work at the stables on Muddypuddle Lane nearly a year ago, after having left her previous position under a bit of a cloud. Neither he nor Petra had expected her to stay long, but she'd fallen in love, and the rest, as they say, is history.

To Amos's consternation, Lena's eyes filled with tears again.

'This will be Mum's last Christmas,' she said. 'I can feel it!' She slapped a hand to her chest, above her heart. 'I wish I could do something to make it special for her. Maybe I could take her to a show, or something?' Lena pulled a face. 'Or maybe not – she was never one for musicals or the theatre. You'll never guess what she said just now: she told me she wants to smell the fresh air and feel the wind on her face, and she wants to see a horse again. As if that's going to happen.'

She sniffed and dabbed at her eyes once more. 'Oh, well, never mind.'

Slowly Amos said, 'Maybe we can work something out? How about if I speak to William and ask if it's possible to bring Olive to the stables? Do you think that will be allowed?'

Lena frowned as she thought. 'I don't see why not. The residents are often taken out on trips if they're up to it. I believe some of them are going to the panto next week.'

'Oh, no, they aren't,' Amos chorused, earning himself a shake of the head from Lena at his pathetic panto-inspired joke.

'Are you sure about this?' she asked.

'Definitely! She can be wheeled into the yard to see the horses close up, if she doesn't mind the cobbles, and the views from there are stunning, as you know.' His eyes suddenly widened as a thought occurred to him. 'Do you think any of the others might enjoy a trip to the stables?'

'I've no idea. Brian might – he was quite taken with Gerald last year.'

'Most people were,' Amos said. 'It's not often a donkey rocks up at Honeymead.'

'I suppose not.' Her expression lightened. 'You looked very convincing in your Santa outfit. Will you dress up as Father Christmas again this year?'

'I'm not sure that's a compliment,' Amos chuckled. 'You're right, though – I **am** old and whiskery, but I'm not as cuddly as Santa.' He patted his stomach, pleased that he only had a small paunch and had had to shove a cushion inside the jacket of his Father Christmas outfit last year to make it look more authentic.

'I think you look very cuddly,' Lena declared, then blushed when she realised how it sounded. 'That didn't come out right. I'm not saying you're overweight. What I meant was… oh, dear!' She looked mortified.

'I do give rather nice cuddles,' Amos said, trying to make her feel better. 'Ask Amory.'

She shot him a grateful smile and changed the subject. 'Do you really think you can arrange for the residents to visit the stables? It's not the sort of place they normally get taken to, and I'm not sure how much they'll get out of it, apart from my mum. She'll love it.'

Lena had a point, Amos thought. It wasn't as though the stables had a tearoom or a cafe, and considering they couldn't wander around the yard, the only thing they'd be able to do would be to sit in the gallery and watch a lesson, or watch Petra lead a couple of ponies around the arena for them to take a gander at. Hardly riveting, was it?

Unless...?

He could always provide mince pies and hot chocolate, and what if Petra put on a mini show, like a kind of gymkhana?

'I've got an idea,' he said, abruptly. 'I'm not going to tell you what it is, because it mightn't get off the ground yet. But if it does...'

'No. Definitely not.' Petra was adamant. She looked horrified. 'What on earth are you thinking? Holding a nativity play at the stables for an audience of care home residents isn't going to work. Admittedly, we've put on nativity plays in the past, but they were just for the parents and were only a bit of fun. Anyway, I've got too much to do as it is, without putting on a damned play.'

'**You** don't have to do anything,' Amos told her. 'October and Charity are more than happy to organise it.' He winced as he said it. He was trying to present Petra with a fait accompli because he knew she wouldn't be keen on the idea, so he had already asked the girls to help, and they had seemed quite keen.

Petra lifted the saddle off Parsnip's back, and steam rose from the pony's coat where it had rested. Scooping up a handful of clean straw, she proceeded to rub his fur dry. At this time of year the pony was as fluffy as a teddy bear, and the exercise, plus his thick winter coat of long cream guard hairs, had made him sweat. Amos guessed that she would probably pop a rug on him before she turned him out into the field for the afternoon.

'**They** might be happy about it, but I'm not,' she said. 'Christmas is only three weeks away. There's not enough time. And even if there was, having a bunch of OAPs in a drafty arena catching their death of cold, isn't a good idea. The viewing gallery isn't at all suitable. And what about those poor souls who can't travel? It's not fair for them to miss out.'

Amos cleared his throat. 'Ah, now, I've thought about that. Luca says he can live stream it.'

Peta narrowed her eyes. 'Am I the last to know about this?'

He knew he was looking sheepish. 'Not quite. I haven't told Nathan yet.'

'Because you know that he'll tell you it's a silly idea, too,' Petra pointed out.

'I haven't spoken to him because he's repairing the dry stone wall at the top of the field by Walter's house, and it's too cold to walk all the way up to Lilac Tree Farm.' Amos blew on his hands as though to demonstrate just how cold it was, but Petra was right and she knew it. He added, 'Megan said she'll bake a cake or two.'

'You've spoken to **Megan**?' Petra's voice rose an octave. Oh, dear...

'I bumped into her in Picklewick.' Amos gave his niece an innocent smile, but he knew she wasn't fooled. The 'bumping' had been pre-planned.

'What does William think?' Petra had a triumphant look on her face, but if she thought she'd won this argument, she was sadly mistaken.

'He thinks it's a great idea.' Amos tried not to smirk. The care home manager had been all for it.

'Then he's even more of an idiot than you,' Petra snapped. In a softer voice, she added, 'It's a lovely idea and a wonderful thing to do, but it's simply not feasible.'

'I thought we could involve some of the children from the local primary school,' Amos continued as though she hadn't spoken. 'They could be the choir.'

Petra finished fastening Parsnip's rug and patted the pony on the neck. 'You've thought of everything, haven't you?'

'I've tried to.'

'Why are you so set on doing this? It's not as though the care home ignores Christmas. They put on lots of things, and you could always take Gerald to see them, like you did last year.'

Suddenly Amos didn't feel so sure of himself, and he shuffled his feet and his gaze dropped to the ground. He wanted to put on a nativity play for the residents of the care home out of the goodness of his heart, but there was another reason –

he had a soft spot for Lena. A very soft spot indeed, and he hated to see her so upset.

'Er, it's because of Olive,' he said.

'Lena's mother?'

'Yes. Lena reckons this will be Olive's last Christmas and she wants to do something special for her. You see, Olive used to ride a lot when she was younger, and she loves hearing me talk about the stables, and Lena said...' He trailed off, heat creeping into his face, as he realised how enthusiastic he sounded.

Petra was scrutinising him intently, and he cleared his throat and scuffed the ground with his foot.

'I've not seen you this animated since the wedding,' she said. 'I was getting worried about you. You seemed to have fallen a little flat lately.'

'Aye, well, maybe I just needed something to get my teeth into,' he mumbled. 'A bit of a project. You know how I like to keep busy.'

He wasn't lying, but he wasn't being strictly truthful either. His enthusiasm was as much to do with Lena, as wanting to give himself something to do.

Petra placed a hand on his arm. 'Okay, if it means that much to you, we'll hold the damned nativity play. But just be careful, eh? I don't want you overdoing it.' She paused and a slow smile spread across her face. 'Say hi to Lena for me, next time you see her.'

Her expression left Amos wondering whether Petra had guessed that he had more than a friendly interest in the woman in question.

CHAPTER TWO

Amos was unaccountably nervous about speaking to Lena this morning.

He thought it might be because he'd had such trouble talking Petra round. Nathan, once he knew about the proposed nativity play, had also added his two-pence worth into the conversation. It had taken a while for Amos to convince the stable manager that it was a good idea, but he'd got there in the end and eventually Nathan had come around to his way of thinking, despite his initial grumpiness that he had enough work to be getting on with at the stables as it was, without adding a last-minute nativity play to his never-ending list of jobs.

Actually, Amos didn't want Nathan's involvement – apart from moving the odd chair and bale of hay – and neither did he want Petra's interference. He wanted to do this himself, with a little help from October and Charity who would sort the ponies out, and a lot of help from Lena. He was going to enjoy spending time with her. **If** she agreed to help, that is. Because he hadn't asked her yet, and there was the possibility that she might say no.

Tentatively, and with his heart in his mouth, he rang her doorbell.

When she opened the door and saw him on the step, she looked taken aback. 'Hello? I thought you were a delivery driver,' she said.

'I am in a way. I'm here to deliver some good news, I hope.'

'You'd better come in.' She stood to the side and held the door open.

Amos went inside and waited for her to close it behind him, then she led him down a small hall and into a living room.

It was alive with colour and lights, and for a moment he was taken aback. This lady certainly did like Christmas. There was a tree in the bay window, which he had noticed when he was dithering about knocking on her door, and a garland was draped around the mantlepiece, which also had twinkling lights threaded through it, illuminating acorns, berries and little felt-covered robins, and some knitted stockings hanging from it. Above the fireplace was a mirror, which was also adorned with a garland with yet more fairy lights, and there were Christmassy ornaments on the mantlepiece itself.

And that was just the start of it.

Through another doorway he saw a dining table which was nearly obliterated by a whole range of decorations and neatly wrapped presents, and he did a double-take.

Lena saw him staring. 'Excuse the mess. I was in the middle of putting the trimmings up.'

'Sorry. I can see you're busy. I'll call back another time.'

'Oh, no, you don't. I'll be on pins for the rest of the day wondering what you wanted. Anyway, I was about to break for some lunch. Would you care to join me?'

'Er...I...um. Yes, please,' he decided. 'I'd like that very much.'

'It's only soup,' she warned.

'I like soup. What kind?'

'Mushroom. I made it myself. And there's some cheesy bread to go with it.'

'Lovely!'

'Come through to the kitchen, and you can tell me why you're here while I heat it up.'

Thankfully the kitchen was devoid of anything Christmas-related, apart from a bowl of nuts with their shells still on them, a nutcracker in the shape of a reindeer, and a festive tea towel. The room was light, modern, and spotlessly clean, unlike the kitchen at the stables. It put him to shame when he thought of the open fireplace, the dogs and cat, the scruffy old armchair, and the clutter that he seemed to be constantly clearing away.

'This is nice,' he said, after Lena had indicated for him to take a seat at a small table in the corner. He sniffed appreciatively as the aroma of garlic and onions began to fill the air. draft

'It's too big for me now that October's moved in with Luca,' she said. 'It's got four bedrooms and two reception rooms, and I'm sick of cleaning them – although they might come in handy when I have grandchildren.'

'Is that on the cards?' October hadn't mentioned anything about being pregnant, and although he would be thrilled for her, Amos hoped the stables wasn't going to lose her just yet.

'I wouldn't be surprised. She and Luca have been together for nearly a year now, so it looks like it's serious. I'm expecting them to get engaged soon.'

'Doesn't time fly? I was only thinking the other day that it'll soon be a year since she started work at the stables.'

Lena ladled soup into a couple of bowls and placed one of them in front of him. She popped the cheesy bread between them on the table and sat down.

Spoon in hand, she said, 'Tuck in, and while you're eating you can share the good news.'

Amos ate a mouthful of soup and closed his eyes in delight. 'This is delicious. You must give me the recipe.'

'Not until you tell me why you're here!' she cried, laughing. 'You can't keep me in suspense like this.'

Amos reached for a slice of bread. 'You know that idea I had yesterday? The one I couldn't tell you about in case it fell through?'

She nodded, her eyes searching his face.

'The stables is going to put on a nativity play and all the residents of Honeymead are invited. William is on board with it, so all we've got to do now is make it happen.'

Lena put her spoon down, resting it on the edge of her bowl. 'When you say **we...?**

'Me and you.' Amos was grinning so widely he thought his face might split in two. 'What do you think?'

'I don't know anything about putting on a play. Are you expecting me to act? I'm a bit old to be Mary, although I'm sure little Amory would make an adorable Baby Jesus, and you do have a donkey you can use.'

'I'm going to ask the kids who come for riding lessons if they would like to be in it. We've laid on nativity plays in the past, so I expect they'll be up for it. What do you think?' he repeated.

'I think it's a lovely idea...'

'But?'

'The arena is freezing. And what about those old folk who are not very mobile?

How are they going to manage in the gallery?'

'I've thought about that,' Amos said, taking another mouthful of the delicious soup. 'Hot water bottles, patio heaters and blankets. Oh, and nicer chairs. Those hard plastic ones are so uncomfortable.'

'Where are you going to get nicer chairs from?'

'William estimates that we will need about twenty-five, and he's got seventeen old ones we can use, as long as we supply the transport – they're in storage in a shed at the moment. We have two up at the house, and we can borrow the rest from the cottages and from...er...you, or Nathan, or anyone who's willing to lend us one really. And some of the old people, like Olive for instance, will be in a wheelchair, so they'll sit in those.'

'You've really thought this through, haven't you?'

'I've tried to think of everything, but I expect I've missed something.'

Lena thought for a moment, then said, 'Let's eat this before it gets cold, then we'll have a chat about it. If we're going to do this, it has to be done properly.'

Amos grinned. She mightn't have said yes, but he simply knew she was going to agree to help. After all, this whole thing was for her mum's benefit.

But giving the folks in the home a nice afternoon was only part of it. The other part was the thought of having Lena with him every step of the way, and he couldn't wait to get stuck in.

When Amos had appeared at her door, telling her he had some news and looking very pleased with himself, Lena had been expecting him to say that he'd arranged to drive her mother up to the stables. Thinking back, she could simply have asked October to give her a hand in getting her mum in and out of the car, especially since she worked there. Lena felt certain there wouldn't have been an issue with having an old lady call in to see a horse or two, so there really wasn't any need to have involved Amos whatsoever.

But when he'd relayed the news that he was planning to put on a nativity play, she had been astonished. It was simultaneously a lovely idea and a worrying one. She had no doubt that the kids would have a wonderful time, but she was concerned about the elderly care home residents. Still, if William was fine with it, then maybe she should be too. He was far more qualified to assess the risks and the needs of the residents in his care, and he was blimmin' good at what he did. She had never heard a single complaint about the home or the way it was run. In fact, it had a reputation for being one of the best in the area, and Lena knew her mum was in excellent hands and was very well cared for.

'Okay,' she began, after she had cleared away the lunch things and Amos had wiped up whilst she'd washed the dishes.

They were sitting at the table with a slice of rich, aromatic Christmas cake in front of them. Lena considered having a mug of hot chocolate to go with it, but thought tea might be better for her waistline. At her age, it was far easier to put weight on, than to take it off.

'We should make a list of everything that needs to be done, the order in which it needs doing, and the timeline,' she began.

Amos blinked owlishly. 'It's all sorted, more or less.'

'It's the **less** bit that concerns me. If you want this to run smoothly, you can't leave anything to chance.'

'It's only a little nativity play.'

'You do realise that relatives may want to come too,' she said. 'Especially the parents of the children taking part.'

Amos blinked again. 'I never thought of that. But that's only a few more people to accommodate, surely?'

'Maybe, and maybe not.' Lena's mind was buzzing with possibilities. Not only did she want to make what was probably her mum's last Christmas extra-special, but she had an idea to help Amos and the stables.

'I was thinking bigger,' she said, and when she told him her idea and saw his face light up, she clapped her hands in delight.

Amos had been looking down in the dumps recently, and this seemed to have perked him up no end. She hadn't liked to admit it, but she had been worried about him. Ever since Petra and Harry's wedding he had seemed subdued, not his usual self, and she'd been concerned that his health might be deteriorating. Seeing him come up with the idea of putting on a nativity play and being so full of enthusiasm for it, warmed her heart. He appeared ten years younger, and she was struck, not for the first time, by how attractive he was for an older man.

He was in his early seventies, nine years older than her, but she supposed he could be described as a silver fox. However, it wasn't his weather-beaten features or upright bearing that was the most attractive thing about him – it was his kindness. He didn't **have** to call into the care home and sit with the old folks a couple of times a month, but he did it anyway out of the goodness of his heart. Neither did he have to put the wheels in motion for a nativity play – once again, it was pure altruism on his part. The stables had nothing to gain from it, apart from a lot of hassle, so when an idea had popped into Lena's head as a way of saying thank you, she leapt on it.

'Right,' she said, pulling a notepad out of a drawer and fetching a pen. 'Shall we work backwards from the event itself, make a list of what needs doing and when it needs doing by, then we can divvy them up.'

Amos was staring at her, concern on his face. 'Are you going to have time for this? I honestly don't mind doing it on my own.'

'Of course I've got time; far too much of it, as it happens.' Since her mum had gone to live in Honeymead, Lena had more time on her hands than she knew what to do with. Visiting Olive every day only took up a couple of hours, and she was often scratching around for things to do. She wished she enjoyed baking, like Megan, but every cake she made turned out flat, and although she pottered in the garden there was a limit to how much weeding, mowing or planting she could do. Besides, it was winter, and she really didn't want to work in the garden in this weather. It would be a welcome change to have something to get her teeth into, and she'd enjoy working with Amos. In fact, she couldn't wait to get stuck in.

'If you don't mind me saying,' Amos began, 'I get the impression you've done this kind of thing before.'

'You could say that,' she chuckled. 'I used to be a project manager for a rather large company. This stuff is second nature to me.'

'If I'd have known that, I would have just mentioned the idea, then let you get on with it. You can clearly do this on your own,' Amos grinned.

She could and she might have done, if not for one thing – she was looking forward to spending time with Amos. And she wasn't entirely sure why, although she did have her suspicions.

Amos was bubbling with excitement as he headed back to the stables. Lena's idea was grander than anything he could have dreamt up himself, and he marvelled that the little nativity play which had originally been meant for a few elderly folk, might become a village-wide affair. It was going to be hard work, and it might prove impossible to pull off in such a short amount of time, but they would give it their best shot.

He and Lena had been hard at it all afternoon, and he'd marvelled at her organisational skills. At one point he had seriously wondered whether he was surplus to requirements, a feeling of déjà vu creeping over him as he thought of how he'd felt yesterday morning when faced with Petra and Harry getting on with things without him, but he had soon changed his mind when she'd issued him with a variety of tasks.

It was too late to start on them today though: he needed to get back to the stables to prepare the evening meal. Briefly he wondered how Petra had managed without his help this afternoon. Had she stayed in the office, working on the accounts, or had she been forced to take the baby with her when she tacked up the ponies that were being used for this evening's lessons? Or did Harry not have any clients today?

Amos felt guilty for abandoning his niece, but he also felt a sense of freedom. He'd had the whole day to himself. It was strange, but not unwelcome. Usually, he was only away for a couple of hours and then he would return, eager to do his bit, conscious that although Petra might run the stables, the business was ultimately his responsibility.

Maybe it was time to hand the reins over to her?

But then again, what would he do with himself all day? The stables was the only thing he'd known for all of his working life.

He hadn't set out to own horses, and he hadn't had any dealings with the creatures at all until he'd met Mags. He had lived in a small town on the east coast with his older brother and parents, and had only really been interested in having fun. But when he'd taken a trip into Great Yarmouth with a group of friends, he had met Margaret. She had been on holiday with her family, and he'd been captivated by her. So much so, that he had slept on the beach that night so he could meet her for breakfast the following morning. Talk about a whirlwind romance! He had followed her halfway across the country to a little village called Picklewick and had married her within six months.

He had been surprised to learn that she lived on a farm with her parents, and he'd been even more surprised to discover that he enjoyed working outside with the animals. But what he really loved (aside from Mags herself) was her horses.

She'd already started offering hacks onto the hills, and gradually the stables side of the farm became more important than the sheep-rearing side, until eventually the stables on Muddypuddle Lane was born. Amos had taken to it like a duck to water, and had been a swift learner, immersing himself in everything and anything to do with horses.

After a period of time Mags's parents passed away, leaving the house and the land to Mags, and she and Amos had run the stables together, a self-contained unit of two. He wished they'd had children but it wasn't to be, and if he was honest, he had been perfectly content with his life as it was – just him and Mags.

Then Mags died and Petra had come into his life, and Amos didn't know what he'd have done without her. She was like a daughter to him even though she was his great-niece, his brother's son's child. The stables would pass to her when the time came, and he knew he would leave it in safe hands, because it already was.

'There you are!' Petra exclaimed, when he stomped into the boot room and shed his waxed cotton jacket and flat cap.

Queenie leant against his legs and politely nudged his hand with her nose, asking to be petted.

Amory wasn't as polite. As soon as he saw Amos he shrieked at the top of his voice and leant towards him, his pudgy little hands opening and closing.

'I think someone is pleased to see you,' Petra said, as she handed the baby over to him for a cuddle.

Amos nuzzled his nose into the infant's fuzzy hair and breathed in the lovely scent of talcum powder and freshly changed baby. He could also smell the aroma of roasting chicken, and he gave an exaggerated sniff and raised his eyebrows.

'What can I smell?' he asked.

'I've put a chicken in the oven,' Petra said. 'I saw it in the fridge and guessed that's what we're having for supper.'

Amos was put out. It was **his** job to do the cooking, not hers. That was the arrangement – Petra saw to all the outside stuff, with the help of Nathan, October and Charity, and he dealt with all the inside things, such as the household chores, the cooking and the paperwork. It seemed he was being usurped at every turn, and he didn't like it.

Abruptly his good mood evaporated.
Maybe he **was** past his sell-by-date, after
all?

CHAPTER THREE

Amos studied the list of tasks and sighed. All yesterday evening and throughout most of the night he had been having second thoughts about the nativity play. It still wasn't too late to change his mind, although he knew he would be letting a few people down – Lena being the most important. Luckily, he hadn't approached any of the children who attended riding lessons at the stables to ask if they would like to be involved, and neither had he spoken to the headteacher of the local primary school. The other good thing was that none of the residents of the care home knew. William might be disappointed, but Amos was sure he wouldn't be too put out. After all, if the nativity play didn't go ahead, William wouldn't have to ferry thirty or so residents up to the stables and back, with all the headache that would entail.

He'd speak to Lena this morning, he vowed, and tell her it was off. He wasn't looking forward to the conversation because he'd seen how enthusiastic she had been, but he was sure she would be alright once he explained the reason why.

Actually, what reason **was** he going to give?

He didn't want to tell her that the reason he had lost heart was because he was starting to feel useless and a burden at the stables. That was hardly a valid reason, was it? But valid reason or not, that was how he felt.

Amos checked the time. It was eleven a.m. and he guessed that at this time in the morning Lena might very well be at the care home. He'd leave it until a little later to pop in and see her, he decided. He could just as easily call her on the phone and tell her, but he thought it would be better face-to-face.

'Have you got any plans for today?' Petra asked as she breezed into the house, bringing a blast of cold air with her. Amos was giving the boot room a bit of a tidy. It was amazing how quickly mess seemed to accumulate. The boot room was an area just off the kitchen where coats were hung, boots were left (hence the name), and where the dog and cat bowls were kept. But it didn't end there: anything and everything usually ended up in this room, from sacks of chicken feed to garden implements. No sooner had he cleared the place out, than new stuff appeared. He supposed it was better than having it migrate into the rest of the house, but still...

Petra had shucked off her coat and was toeing off her Wellington boots. Queenie and Patch, Nathan's small terrier, were already heading for their usual spot in front of the fire, where Tiddles was already sleeping. The cat opened one gimlet eye, gave the dogs a threatening glare which they ignored, and went back to sleep.

'Amos? I asked if you've got anything planned for today?' Petra repeated.

His thoughts flew to Lena. 'Not really. Why, did you have something particular in mind that you want me to do?'

'Yes and no. Nathan will be doing the heavy lifting, but I need you to decide where it's to go.'

'Where's what to go?'

'The Christmas tree,' Petra said. 'I've usually put it up by now, but I'm glad I didn't because we'll need to locate it with the nativity play in mind.'

'About that…' He ground to a halt.

Petra had finally got her wellies off, revealing three pairs of thick socks. She kicked the boots into the corner, spotted the stern expression on his face, retrieved them and placed them neatly side by side underneath the row of jackets and coats hanging on the wall.

'Sorry,' she said. 'Hello, sweetie.'

This was addressed to Amory, who was in his bouncy chair gurgling happily. The baby chortled when he saw his mum.

'I thought I'd see if he wanted a quick feed, and have a cup of tea while I was here. And then we could go into the arena and work out where you want to put the tree. I don't think where we had it last year would work, not if we're going to have loads of people in the gallery all at the same time, because it would spoil their view. I was thinking about the far corner. It would make a nice backdrop, but I'll leave it up to you to decide.'

Petra seemed quite on board with the idea of the nativity play and Amos pulled a face. How could he now tell her that it wasn't going ahead? Especially since she and Nathan had taken quite a bit of convincing. He neither did he want to share the real reason with her. He knew how he felt and that his feelings were valid, but he feared that by saying them aloud he would sound daft.

'Wherever you think is best,' he said.

'Oh no, you're not leaving this one with me,' Petra stated firmly. 'This is your idea, so you're going to have to sort everything out. I've got enough to be getting on with.' She was smiling as she said it, but he knew she was right. She really did have enough to be getting on with.

She could be doing without all this, he thought. Although she had told him that the nativity play was his responsibility, he suspected she would nevertheless fret and worry about it, even if it was from behind the scenes. His niece had always been a bit of a control freak, which was a good thing considering that she now had two businesses to juggle, plus a baby. Was it fair on him to add yet another burden? In fact, it would be the perfect excuse not to go ahead with it. Petra might argue a bit, but he suspected she'd be pleased.

He was about to tell her his decision, when the phone rang. Petra had just picked the baby up and was unbuttoning her shirt ready to give the little boy a feed, so Amos hurried to answer it.

'Hello, you're through to the stables on Muddypuddle Lane. How can I help?' There was always a pad and a pen next to the phone, and he picked up the pen in readiness.

'Amos?' It was Lena on the other end.

'Hi, Lena, I was going to pop over to see you later,' he began, but her excited voice cut through what he was going to say.

'I've just been on the phone to The Picklewick Paper,' she said in a rush, 'and they're very keen on covering the nativity play. They think it's a great idea, and they reckon it's the sort of thing their readers love at Christmas.'

'I see,' Amos said, his thoughts whirling.

'And I've also spoken with the headteacher of Picklewick Primary and she said she'd love to bring some of her pupils to sing a few carols. They're already doing rehearsals for the carol service on Christmas Eve in the church, so she said it's not any trouble. She sounded delighted, and she agreed that loads of parents and grandparents would want to come. She also said she would ask the children to make some flyers to advertise it.'

'Advertise it?'

'Yes, you know —leaflets that the pupils can take home to show their parents. If we're going to ask for donations to charity on the day, we're going to want as many people as possible to come. Have you spoken to Megan yet?'

'Um, no, not yet.' One of his tasks was to have a chat with Megan about making a Christmas cake to raffle, although he had already sounded her out about making cakes and mince pies to eat on the day. He was also supposed to be tapping up a shopkeeper or two in the village for more raffle prizes. 'Er, Lena—?'

'Is that Lena on the phone? Tell her I said hi,' Petra called as she walked past on the way upstairs, Amory in her arms.

'Say hi back for me,' Lena said. 'Sorry, I've got to go, there's someone at the door. Speak later. Bye.'

Amos stood there, holding a dead phone and wondering what had just happened.

'How's her mum?' Petra asked from halfway up the stairs.

'What? Er, oh...still the same, I think.' The speed with which Lena had moved was breathtaking.

'What did she want?'

'Just to update me on a few things to do with the nativity play.' Bugger! He could hardly back out now, not when Lena had already got the ball rolling. It was more than rolling, it was bouncing down a hill at breakneck speed.

'She's helping you, is she?'

'Um, yeah. Didn't I say?'

Petra smirked. 'No, you didn't.'

Crossly Amos slapped the phone down on the hall table. He caught sight of himself in the mirror above it and rolled his eyes at his reflection. It looked like the nativity play was going ahead whether he wanted it to or not.

'I'm just going to pop Amory into his snowsuit, then we'll go to the arena, yeah?' she said, resuming her climb to the first floor. Then she paused again. 'How about inviting Lena to the stables for supper this evening, and the pair of you can fill me in on what's going on –

because I have a feeling there's more to this little nativity play than meets the eye.'

If only she knew the half of it, he thought with a resigned sigh.

Amos reached for the phone again...Petra was going to do her nut!

At least organising the nativity play was helping take her mind off her mum, Lena thought, as she dashed home to get changed. She had spent the afternoon at the nursing home, spending some time with her mother and the rest of it with various members of staff, William especially.

The whole thing had grown from a simple visit to the stables for a mince pie and a hot chocolate whilst watching some of the young riders put on a little play, to an event of epic proportions. She knew she had hijacked Amos's idea and it had run away with her a bit, but she couldn't seem to help it. She kept telling herself that she was doing this for her mum, but she had a sneaking suspicion she was doing it more for her own benefit. Lena wanted her mother's last Christmas to be special for several reasons – the main one was because Lena wanted to treasure the memory, but she was realistic enough to know that by keeping busy she was also keeping her fear of not having her mother around for much longer at bay.

What was she going to do without her? Lena had moved to Picklewick a decade ago to care for Olive when it became clear that she was struggling to live on her own, and Lena had looked after her ever since. Even though Olive was living at Honeymead now, Lena still spent a proportion of each day with her, because what else was she going to do with her time?

That was something else she was scared of – being alone. She had October, but her daughter was getting on with her own life. She had a job she loved and a man she adored, and although she made time for Lena, her mother wasn't October's priority. Which meant that when Olive passed, Lena's days would be all the emptier. And incredibly lonely.

Lena had already started to feel the bite of loneliness since her mum had moved into the care home last year, but she guessed that was nothing compared to the loneliness she would feel when she no longer had her mum to visit.

'Stop being so maudlin,' she muttered to herself as she rounded the corner into her street and spotted the festive lights twinkling in the windows of her little house. She had finished trimming up and was pleased with the results, even if she was the only one who would get to appreciate them. They always served to cheer her up, and her spirits lifted at the sight of them.

They lifted even more once she was inside and saw the full effect. No wonder Amos had done a double-take when he'd entered her living room. It was quite something, even if she did say so herself.

The Christmas decorations weren't the only reason she was feeling a little more chipper than of late. She had been invited to supper at the stables. Amos had phoned her this morning, to ask if she'd like to join them for their evening meal to discuss how the plans were coming along. Lena knew the invitation was for purely functional reasons because there was a great deal to do in a rather short space of time, but it was so rare for her to go out in the evening these days that she was really looking forward to it. It was also a treat to have a meal cooked for her, because since her mum had moved out, Lena sometimes simply couldn't be bothered to cook for herself.

'What do you mean **sometimes**?' she mumbled aloud, as she trotted upstairs to have a wash and to put on fresh clothes. **Often**, was more accurate. The toaster had become a firm friend, as had the ready meal section in the supermarket. And, to her shame, even heating one of those had become a bit of a chore. However, she had made some soup recently she recalled, and she would have had enough for a couple of meals if Amos hadn't helped her eat it. It had been rather fortuitous that she had been in a cooking mood that day.

She knew that Amos did the majority of the cooking at the stables, and she also knew he was good at it. Barbeque food, at least – he'd fired up the barbie (as the Aussies say) when many of the villagers had got together earlier in the year to help Petra clear the old cow shed ready for the builders to move in and turn it into three lovely holiday cottages.

Now, should she wear a dress, Lena wondered, opening her wardrobe door and peering inside. Or would that be too formal? She didn't want to look as though she was going to a fancy restaurant. But neither did she want to look as though she'd not made an effort.

A sudden realisation made her pause.

Who was she making the effort for?

Lena tried to convince herself that it was for her, but she knew deep down that it wasn't. She wanted to make an effort for **Amos**.

Oh, my...where had that idea come from?

Lena edged backwards until she felt the back of her knees touch the mattress, then she plopped onto the bed, the springs bouncing under her weight.

Amos, she mused, her mind filled with images of him – playing Santa Claus at the care home last Christmas, waving a fork around as he cooked burgers and sausages at the cow shed clearing, the stricken look on his face when Petra had gone into labour early, the way he gave each resident at the care home his full attention when he spoke to them...

He was a lovely man. Very kind, extremely thoughtful. And, despite having his family around him, Lena suspected he might be lonely. His wife, Mags, had died before Lena had moved to Picklewick, but Lena had heard that the two of them had been inseparable and that Amos had been devastated at her loss. He must miss her dreadfully still.

There was something else that Lena had become aware of, and it had only just hit her, which was why she'd had to sit down.

Not only was Amos a thoroughly nice man, he was also a handsome one. A

very handsome one. One that she would like to see more of.

Considering she had been man-free for so many years, Lena felt quite giddy at the unaccustomed attraction she was feeling, and she had absolutely no idea what she should do about it.

That was lovely, Lena thought, as she ate the last mouthful on her plate, and she wasn't just referring to the meal, which had been delicious and cooked by Amos's own fair hands. Actually his hands were large and strong-looking and she wondered how they would feel on her— Stop it!

'Everything alright, Lena?' Amos wore a concerned expression.

'Yes, why?'

'You made a kind of groaning noise.'

Lena felt heat rush into her cheeks. 'Did I? Sorry. I was just thinking how delightfully full I am. I don't think I could eat another morsel.'

'Thank goodness for that! I thought I'd poisoned you.' He grinned at her. 'Does that mean I can't tempt you with a portion of chocolate pavlova with spiced pears?'

'Oh, go on, then. I'm sure I can manage some. It sounds yummy.'

'It is,' Petra said. 'I can vouch for that. Amos is a darned good cook. He'll make someone a wonderful husband.'

Lena assumed Petra was joking until she noticed Amos colouring up, then she caught Petra's eye and saw that Petra was grinning at her.

Lena didn't know where to put herself. Was that comment aimed at her? Or was she reading too much into it?

If it hadn't been for her realisation earlier that she was starting to develop a crush on the stables' owner, Lena wouldn't have thought twice. But here she was, thinking that Petra was right – Amos **would** make some lucky woman a wonderful husband. However, she was fairly sure he wasn't in the market for a wife.

And neither did she want a husband. She'd come close to it with October's father but it hadn't happened, and she was far too old to consider sharing her life now.

A little voice inside her head muttered about ending up a lonely old maid, but she ignored it. She was already an old maid, and she'd just have to find something to occupy her to stop her from getting lonely, wouldn't she.

Dessert tasted as wonderful as it sounded, and by the time she had spooned up the last mouthful, Lena really did feel like groaning. She was fit to burst and wished she had worn a looser pair of trousers. Saying that though, the ones she was wearing had been loose enough when she'd put them on a couple of hours ago.

Amos got to his feet to collect the dirty dishes and when Petra tried to help, he waived her away. 'You and Harry go have a check around and make sure everything is bedded down for the night. I can manage.'

'With my help.' Lena added. 'You don't think I'm just going to sit here and watch you clean up!'

'You're a guest,' Amos protested.

'Nonsense! I'm an old friend.'

'That you are,' Amos agreed, beaming at her. 'Not as old as me though!'

'When you get to be as old as we are, age is just a number.'

'Hmm.' Amos didn't look convinced, so she hastened to reassure him.

'You don't look a day over sixty,' she said. 'It must be all the fresh air and good food. Petra is right, you are a good cook.'

'I've got to do something to earn my keep,' he said. His tone was light, but Lena sensed something was bothering him.

'I think you probably do plenty,' she said.

'Not enough,' he muttered as he ran a bowlful of hot water.

Lena moved the pile of stacked dishes closer to the sink and looked around for a tea towel. 'Want to talk about it?'

Amos sighed. 'It's nothing.'

'It must be something for you to look like a cat that's lost her kittens.'

Amos barked out a laugh then sobered. 'It's just...I think...Oh, forget it. I'm just being a daft old codger,' he said.

'You are not a codger, daft or otherwise. And neither are you old. Seventy... what is it? One, two?'

'Three. I'm seventy-three.'

'Seventy-three isn't old. Seventy is the new fifty, apparently.'

'I wish! I feel more like ninety, these days.'

'As I said, you don't look your age, and neither do you act it.'

'Thank you for saying so,' Amos said, but he still seemed down in the dumps.

Clearly he didn't want to talk about it, but if he knew that he wasn't alone, he might open up to her. The animation which he had displayed while they were talking about the nativity play and the progress made in such a short amount of time, had leaked away, and she couldn't help but wonder why.

Conscious that it was none of her business and that she shouldn't pry, Lena nevertheless wanted to do what she could to help, even if it was only offering a shoulder to cry on.

'It's me who should be thanking you,' she began.

 'Nonsense, Olive and the others deserve to have a great Christmas. Anyway, you're doing most of the work.'

'That's not why I'm thanking you,' Lena said, amused. 'Or rather it is, but I also want to thank you on behalf of myself. I've...erm...been a little down lately, and not just because I know I'm going to lose my mum soon.' Lena blinked, trying not to cry. 'You see, I've been rather lonely and at a bit of a loose end since she went into Honeymead, and I think I might have lost my way. This nativity play has given me something to focus on.'

Amos had stopped scrubbing a particularly stubborn pot and was gazing at her sympathetically. 'What will happen when Christmas is over?'

'I've no idea,' she replied truthfully. At the moment she was struggling to see past the nativity play. Or maybe she simply didn't want to. 'You're lucky having Petra and Harry living with you, and little Amory of course. I'll just carry on being lonely, I suppose.'

Amos continued to gaze at her, his expression intense. 'Can I let you into a secret? I'm lonely, too. Oh, I know what you're thinking – how can I possibly be lonely with my family around me? But I can, and I am. I feel surplus to requirements some days.'

Lena gasped. 'Petra isn't trying to kick you out of your own home, is she?'

'Gracious me, no! Nothing like that.' He looked so shocked at the idea that Lena believed him.

'You know I've got angina?' he said, and when she nodded, he carried on. 'I'm doing okay, as long as I keep taking the tablets and don't overdo things.'

He turned his attention back to scrubbing the pot, Lena hanging on his every word.

'The deal is that I do all the indoor stuff, like taking care of the chores, doing the cooking, and seeing to the bookings and the accounts, plus the shopping, pottering in my veggie patch, and since Amory came along, doing a fair bit of babysitting during the day. All this frees up Petra to see to the horses, teach the lessons, and so on. But lately...' He trailed off, and Lena noticed that his eyes were suspiciously damp.

'She has been doing some of the things that you usually do?' Lena guessed.

When Amos shrugged, she knew she'd hit the nail on the head. 'Is that so bad?' she asked gently. 'She probably thinks she's saving you a job.'

'I expect she does, but it makes me feel useless.'

'Is that why you've not been your usual bouncy self lately?'

'I'm never bouncy,' Amos objected.

'But you have been a bit down,' she persisted. 'I thought you might be ill.'

'No more than usual. You haven't been your usual sunny self either, but then how can you be when you're worried about your mum?'

'We're a fine pair, aren't we?' she smiled, holding her hand out for the recently washed saucepan. 'Where does this live?'

'In that cupboard, there.'

Lena gave it a quick wipe and popped it inside.

'I miss my wife,' he said suddenly, and Lena froze. 'I thought time was supposed to be a great healer, but I miss her more with each passing day. Seeing how happy Petra and Harry are just makes it worse. Does that make me a bad person?'

'It makes you human,' Lena replied gently.

'I remember how we were together and...' He stopped again. 'I miss someone of my own to cuddle up to, someone with the same frames of reference as me.'

Lena stroked him on the arm, unable to think of anything to say that might make him feel even a tiny bit better. She couldn't begin to imagine what he was going through.

'Has there been a special someone in your life?' he asked, his voice low.

'There was once – October's father – but it never came to anything. I can barely remember what he looks like now. How awful is that!'

'I wonder sometimes if it's better to have loved and lost, than never to have loved at all.' She envied the love that Amos and Mags had shared, even if the price of that love was the pain he still suffered.

'So do I.' Her reply was heartfelt. 'When October was little and even after she'd grown up, I was so busy with work that I didn't have time for a relationship.'

'And now?'

'Now?' She drew in a slow breath. 'I believe it's far too late. That ship has sailed long ago.'

Anyway, there was no one she could even contemplate having any kind of a relationship with. Then her gaze was drawn to the man standing at the sink, up to his elbows in hot, soapy water, and she thought that maybe there was...

However, even after all this time, Amos still only had eyes for his wife.

'I miss you, Mags. You don't know how bad it can get. It hurts me here. 'Amos thumped himself on the chest. 'And I'm not talking about the angina either, so get that out of your pretty little head.'

He replaced her photo on the bedside cabinet and gently stroked his wife's cheek with his finger. It was his favourite snap of her, taken when she wasn't looking at the camera but staring at something off to her left (he couldn't remember what) and her face was alive with laughter.

They had been so young back then, so full of hopes and dreams, and although some of those had failed to materialise (children, for instance) they had been so very happy together.

Mags had been beautiful too, even to the very end, when she'd been—

Gah! He didn't want to think of her that way. He wanted to remember her when she was young and full of life. Just as he used to be. But now he was old, and life was carrying on without him.

Still, he had enjoyed himself this evening, he thought, as he changed into his pyjamas. But having Lena sitting at the table in the very chair where Mags used to sit, had brought memories of his wife sharply into focus. Especially since he'd been talking about her to Lena. Although he talked to Mags's photo every night, many weeks would go by when no one else spoke her name, and he sometimes wondered whether she had been nothing more than a figment of his imagination.

'I hope I haven't scared poor Lena off,' he said, his gaze shooting to the photo again. 'She must think I'm a miserable old git. She's nice, you'd like her.'

Mags and Lena would have got on like a house on fire, he knew. Although he didn't know Lena very well, he had a feeling she and his wife were similar in many respects, both of them with a no-nonsense, get-on-with-it attitude, hiding a soft heart.

'She told me that Petra just thinks she's saving me a job. I still feel like a spare wheel, though,' and he smiled, hearing Mag's voice in his head telling him not to be such a daft sod.

'Yeah, I know I'm putting on a nativity play, so I can't be that useless, but so far, it's Lena who has done the lion's share of the work.'

Amos thought back to the conversation he'd had with Lena whilst they were clearing up. Had she been telling the truth when she said that helping to organise the play was giving her something to focus on? He knew she was worried about her mum, and for good reason, but Lena had always seemed so capable and together.

'It just goes to show that you can't go by appearances,' he said sadly. 'I would never have guessed she is lonely.'

He had just clambered into bed and was about to put out the light when he could have sworn he heard Mags whisper, 'As are you, my love, as are you.'

CHAPTER FOUR

If Mags were here, what would she do? Amos was standing in one of the outbuildings, thinking. If the shoe was on the other foot and she was alive and he was dead, what would she do?

He'd had the most dreadful night's sleep last night because he'd lain awake for most of it thinking about his wife. He'd mourned her for over a decade, never once looked at another woman since he'd lost her. He'd not wanted to. But now...

His emotions were all over the place and he didn't know what to think or how to make sense of how he was feeling.

However, this morning his first and foremost worry was Petra.

It wasn't fair for her and Harry to have to tiptoe around him. They needed their own space to be a couple, and not falling over him every time they turned around.

Until recently Petra and Amos had rubbed along together quite nicely in the farmhouse, each of them with their distinct and separate roles. Okay, so things did overlap occasionally, namely when Amos couldn't help interfering. Which was why he was relegated to the house and the garden most of the time, because he couldn't be trusted not to do something strenuous, like lift a bale of hay for instance. He knew Petra worried about him, but sometimes he just had to prove to himself that he wasn't a total invalid.

However, he might have been naive to think that nothing would change once Petra married Harry.

Everything had changed. For the better, he hastened to add. Without Harry, there would be no Amory, and no holiday cottages. And Petra wouldn't be happier than Amos could ever remember her being. He was so thankful that Harry had taken over old Ted's farrier business, because if he hadn't, Petra would still be lonely and alone. Not that she had ever admitted it, but he'd been able to tell. She had been adamant that she was perfectly happy with her life the way things were. But when Amos compared the Petra of then to the Petra of now, there was such a marked difference that it made him want to weep. These days she was glowing, joy shining out of her.

Amos remembered when he used to feel like that. When Mags was alive, every day had been a blessing, and he was so thankful for the time he'd had with her. They had been a unit, him and her, self-contained and not needing anyone else.

And this was the reason he was worried about Petra. Neither she nor Harry deserved to have him skulking around like the ghost of Christmas Past. They needed their own space to be a proper family, and they weren't getting it with him in the way.

It was definitely time he seriously thought about moving out of the old farmhouse. It would be a wrench to leave it, because he had lived in it for most of his adult life. It was full of memories of Mags, but now it needed to be full of memories of Petra and her growing family. Amos could take his memories with him. They lived in his head and in his heart. He didn't have to be in the farmhouse to remember his wife. Flipping heck, all he needed to do was close his eyes and there she was.

The question was, where was he to go?

It was because he was pondering this very thing, that he was now standing in one of the old outbuildings, the one that was currently used to store all those bits and pieces that farmers everywhere seem to accumulate, from broken pieces of equipment to old water troughs, to bits of wood, and everything in between. One of the reasons farmers tended to hoard things was because they never knew when something would come in handy.

Another reason was that it was such a pain to get rid of it. He remembered clearing out the rubbish from the old cowshed, and as he stood there scanning the interior of this particular outbuilding, he noticed that quite a number of the items from the cowshed had ended up in here.

The outbuilding had originally been a feed store, and was built from the same stone as the farmhouse and the cowshed. It was in pretty good nick actually. It probably needed repointing, and no doubt it would need a new roof, but it was sizable, and if he put a door there and a window here, and a few partition walls obviously, it would make a very nice dwelling. A bungalow, that's what he was thinking, because he wasn't getting any younger. At his age he had to be practical and plan for the future. How much longer would he be able to negotiate the steep stairs in the farmhouse? How much longer would he be able to lever himself in and out of the bath?

A bungalow with wide doors just in case he needed a walker, a generous bathroom with one of those wet room showers, and a bath that was more suited to his advanced years, would be the sort of things he should be thinking about.

He would still be able to potter up to the house if he was needed of course, although thinking back over the past week or so, it seemed that he would be needed less and less. He could continue to do the accounts, the ordering, and the bookings, but only if Petra and Harry wanted him to.

Petra wasn't aware that he had overheard her chatting to Harry, but he had, and their conversation had been playing on his mind. Harry was a farrier, but as this year progressed, he had been doing less and less blacksmithing, and more and more helping out at the stables. With two businesses to run, Petra had a lot to contend with, so Harry was talking about selling his farrier business.

Amos thought it was a brilliant idea. But he was realistic enough to know that with Harry on site all day, every day, his own role would likely to be even more reduced. And actually, he was okay with that now. Talking to Mags had helped. And so had talking to Lena.

To think that she felt as lonely as he! He never would have guessed. He was lucky: if he did move into the old feed shed, he would still be at the stables and he would still have company if he wanted it. Lena, bless her, no longer had anyone living at home now that her mum had gone into Honeymead, and October had moved in with Luca.

Thinking of Lena, brought him to his other worry.

Actually, it was not so much of a worry, as a revelation.

Mags was right, he **was** lonely.

'What should I do, my darling?' Amos paused as though listening, and stuffed his hands into the pockets of his trousers, hunching down into his jacket.

He knew what he would tell her, if their situations were reversed. He would tell her that she had to start living again. That he would hate to think of her mourning him day after day. That she had too much love to give, to keep it locked in her heart. And that was what she would say to him, he knew it. In fact, she had said those very words not long before she died.

'Promise me you won't grieve forever,' she had breathed, her voice weak and barely there. 'Promise me you will find someone else to love.'

They were almost the last words she had said to him, and it was the last promise he had made to her.

But he hadn't kept it, had he?

He had wrapped his heart in sadness and grief, and told himself that this was the way his life would be from now on.

But these past few days (longer than that, if he was honest) he had started seeing

Lena in a different light, and he could slowly feel the frozen depths of his soul thawing as his feelings for her grew.

It scared the daylights out of him.

He wasn't ready to move on, no matter what his heart was telling him.

Anyway, Lena didn't think of him in that way, so he'd just have to be content with being friends.

Lena looked up as a figure walked into the day room, and her face broke into a wide smile as she saw who it was.

'Look, Mum, October has popped in to see you. Isn't that nice?'

October closed the distance in two strides, and plonked a sloppy kiss on her grandmother's cheek. 'Hiya, Granny. Have you had your hair done?'

'You have, haven't you? Just this morning,' Lena said.

'I've got a voice in my head. I can speak for myself,' Olive snorted crossly.

October sent Lena a sympathetic smile. 'You certainly can, Granny,' she said, dropping down into the chair next to her.

Lena quelled a sigh. She had been trying to cheer her mother up all morning, but nothing was working, not even this unexpected visit from October.

'You'll never guess what Princess did,' October said. 'She only went and—'

I don't care,' Olive interrupted.

'Pardon?' October's eyebrows shot up.

'You heard.' Olive turned away and stared out of the window, her lips pursed.

October mouthed, 'What's up with her?' but all Lena could do was shake her head.

'Shall I fetch us all a nice cup of tea?' Lena suggested. 'October, will you help me carry them?'

'No problem – did you know they've got gingerbread men and mince pies in the cafe, and I spied a bowl of marshmallows to go on top of hot chocolate. Would you like a hot chocolate instead, Granny?'

Olive refused to answer, and the only sign that she had heard was a further tightening of her lips.

'Okay, then.' October made a face. 'A cup of tea coming up.'

As soon as they were out of the room, October said, 'I thought Granny would be pleased about the nativity play.'

'I haven't told her yet. None of the residents know. Amos and I wanted to make sure we had all our ducks in a row before William told them. I'd hate for the play to be announced and for something to go wrong, and it not to take place.'

'What could go wrong?'

'Bad weather, for one thing.'

'But nothing else, surely?'

'Hopefully not. Ooh, that hot chocolate does look nice.' Lena's eyes were drawn to a wizened old lady sitting at one of the tables with a giant mug of hot chocolate in front of her. It was oozing with whipped cream, marshmallows and tiny gold balls.

'Can I make you one?' Rose, the office manager asked. 'They're proving to be very popular.'

'I bet they are! Go on, then, I'd love one, please,' Lena said.

'October? And how about Olive? Would she like one?'

October grinned. 'How can I say no? But I think Granny would prefer tea. I'll fetch it, while you see to the hot chocolates.'

October wandered off in the direction of the hot water dispenser, leaving Lena with Rose.

'What are you doing for Christmas?' Rose asked. 'Apart from organising the event of the year!'

'I was hoping to have lunch here. The kitchen put on a lovely feast last year.'

'I'll put your name down, shall I?'

'Please.' Honeymead allowed visitors to share meals with the residents as long as the care home was given enough notice, which was a wonderful touch and meant a lot to the old folk and their families. Lena would have lunch with her mum, then go home and cook another meal for herself and October to enjoy later.

Oh, wait...

'October, what are you doing for Christmas lunch?' Lena called to her.

'Er...'

Lena saw the panicked expression on her daughter's face, and said, 'It's okay, I understand. You'll want to spend your first Christmas with Luca in your own home.'

'Do you mind? We'll pop over to see you in the morning.'

'That's fine. I'm having lunch here with Granny anyway, so it'll save me having to cook.'

Last year October had just moved back to Picklewick and was staying with Lena, so the two of them had eaten turkey with all the trimmings later in the day, after Lena had returned from the care home. She'd never felt so stuffed in all her life, having eaten two Christmas lunches, so in a way she was pleased that this year she'd only have to eat the one. Still, she knew she'd be lonely with the rest of the afternoon and evening ahead of her with only the telly for company.

There was no way she was going to let on though – she didn't want October to feel guilty. Her daughter had her own life to lead; Lena couldn't expect to be involved in everything, and at least she was seeing both October and her mum on Christmas day, which was more than could be said for some people, who might not see a single soul.

Her thoughts went to Amos who, despite having his family around him, would also be feeling lonely. It was depressing how one could be in a roomful of people and still be alone, she thought.

After she'd finished here, she'd give him a call to thank him for inviting her to supper last night.

'What are you doing right now?' Amos asked when Lena phoned to thank him for supper. It was a nice gesture and he appreciated it.

'Nothing. Why? Did you need me for something?'

'I was wondering if you'd like to meet me in The Black Horse for a bite to eat? I'm popping into the village, and I thought I'd treat myself to a pub lunch. Petra and Harry are having a takeaway this evening, and I'm not too keen on curry, so...What do you say?'

'I'd love to. What time?'

'About half an hour?'

'Great. I'll see you there.'

Amos rubbed his hands together with glee. This would be a rare treat indeed.

Lunch out with a beautiful woman who he liked more than was good for him, wasn't to be sneezed at.

'Petra?' he called as he lifted the keys to the Land Rover off the peg in the kitchen. 'I'm just going into Picklewick for some bits and pieces. Will you be okay for a few hours?'

'Just how many bits and pieces are you planning on getting? Or are you going to the care home as well?'

'I'm popping into The Black Horse actually. I'm taking Lena out for lunch.'

Petra's eyebrows rose so far up her forehead that they almost disappeared into her hairline.

'Don't look at me like that,' he warned. 'It's just a quick bite to eat to discuss the play.'

'I thought we'd discussed everything last night?'

'Yes, well, Lena and I need to finalise some details.'

Petra smirked. 'You like her.'

'Don't start on me with your matchmaking tricks. It won't work. Lena and I are just friends.'

'But I reckon you'd like to be more.'

'You can reckon all you want. I don't need another woman in my life. Your Aunt Mags was the only woman for me.'

'Amos...' Petra began quietly. 'She's been gone a long time. Don't you think—?'

'No, I do not.' Amos felt heat flood into his face.

'I was just thinking—'

'You can jolly well stop thinking. If there's any thinking to be done, I can do it myself.'

'You don't fool me, Amos. I can tell you're not happy.'

'I haven't been happy for years. Not since I lost my Mags.'

'Isn't it about time you were?'

'And you think Lena Rees will make me happy, do you?'

'She might.'

Amos was bristling worse than a hedgehog facing a fox. How dare Petra try to tell him he should be happy. Just because she was all loved up, didn't give her any right to comment on his happiness or otherwise. And why did she think Lena could ever replace Mags in his heart?

As though Petra had read his mind, she said, 'There's room in your life for both of them – Lena and Mags. Do you think I'd stop loving Amory if I had another baby?'

'Don't be daft. Love doesn't work like that.'

'Exactly!'

'This is different.'

'How?'

'Because I don't **want** anyone else. I'm too old for all this romance nonsense.'

'You're never too old for love.'

'I don't love Lena and she sure as hell doesn't love me.'

'Yeah, I know...you're just friends.' Petra fell silent; her gaze locked with his, and he saw the concern and love in her eyes.

'Thank you,' he said, after a while.

'For what?'

'For not telling me that Mags wouldn't want me to be on my own forever.'

'I don't need to. You already know that.' She looked away and took a deep breath. 'I'd better go. Amory is in his chair in the living room watching the lights on the Christmas tree flash on and off. I'm surprised it's kept him entertained for this long.'

Amos said, 'I've left the Indian takeaway menu out. It's next to the fruit bowl. I thought you and Harry could have a curry tonight.'

'Good idea.' She stepped towards him and kissed his cheek. 'I just want you to be happy,' she said. 'It breaks my heart to know you're not.'

'Get away with you. I'm alright.'

'Before I go, do you remember when Harry first came into our lives, and you told me not to leave it too late?'

'I do. You took my advice, I'm delighted to say.'

'How about taking it yourself? You said that finding love is the only thing that truly matters. If you spend your life alone, you'll miss out on so much.'

'I did find love: I had your Aunt Mags,' he repeated.

'I know, but you and Lena could be good together, if you let yourself.'

'She doesn't think of me like that,' he insisted. 'We've known each other for years.'

'But you haven't known her that well, have you, not until these past couple of weeks. All I'm saying is, don't close your mind to the possibility. And don't leave it too late to tell her how you feel, eh?' She squeezed his shoulder. 'Enjoy your meal.'

Amos fervently hoped that he would – because all he could think about was Lena and his growing feelings for her. Petra was right, and Mags was right. He didn't want to live out his remaining years alone. He wanted someone of his own to love and cherish, who would love and cherish him back.

And he was beginning to hope that person might be Lena Rees.

CHAPTER FIVE

'You had better give these out,' Lena said, shoving a sheaf of papers into Amos's hand and standing back warily. It was a long time since she had been this close to a horse and being in the arena up at the stables with at least ten of the large creatures hemming her in, was a bit unnerving.

She never used to be this nervous around horses – heck, she used to ride regularly when she was young. Olive had taught her, and she'd also taught October. Lena used to blame her mother for October's obsession with anything equine. She still did, but at least her daughter was now living nearby and not on the other side of the country, as was the case when October had been chasing her dream of being a professional showjumper and living at whichever yard she happened to be employed by. Lena had lost count of the number of Christmas Days that she'd spent without seeing her daughter, so she was grateful that at least she'd get to see her on Christmas morning this year, even if she would have to spend the rest of the day on her own.

She caught October's eye and smiled warmly. Lena knew that she was luckier than many people, and she had spent last night counting her blessings and telling herself not to be so miserable.

Looking at the bright and expectant faces around her this afternoon, Lena definitely wasn't miserable, although she was apprehensive that this first rehearsal went well. It was going to be a rather novel and unusual take on the nativity play for there to be so many ponies around, but the main actors would be safely on the ground, in the more traditional manner.

Petra, bless her, had done the preliminary work of choosing who should play the key roles, such as Mary and Joseph, so Lena was spared that, and Harry and Nathan had borrowed a piano from the grandma of one of the young riders and had already carted it into the arena.

Conscious that they had less than two weeks to pull this off, Lena clapped her hands and called for silence.

'Right,' she said. 'This is the order in which things are going to happen. The manger and the stable will be set up over there,' she pointed, 'and the inn scene will take place here. Before that, Mary will be led into the arena on Gerald. Are you sure he can take her weight?' Lena asked Petra. She was concerned about the little donkey's back, especially since he was getting on a bit and hadn't been ridden for yonks.

Petra nodded. 'Heidi weighs less than a wet puppy.' She pointed to a pretty girl of around eight or nine, who was as thin as a whippet. 'She won't be on him long, ten minutes at the most. He'll be fine and it's about time the greedy creature earned his keep.'

'Okay,' Lena nodded. 'Joseph— Who's playing Joseph?'

A boy's hand shot up.

'What's your name? Actually, don't tell me, I'll only forget,' Lena said. 'I'll call you Joseph. So, Joseph, you'll lead Gerald with Mary on his back into the arena, after you hear the last bars of **O Little Town of Bethlehem**. You'll walk over to the innkeeper and ask for a room for the night. Who's playing the innkeeper?'

Another hand was raised, this time by a girl.

'We've got more girls than boys taking lessons,' Petra explained.

'No problem. Who said the innkeeper had to be male anyway? It could just as easily have been a woman. Anyway, where was I? Oh, yes, I remember...The innkeeper will tell Joseph that there are no rooms, and direct him and Mary to the stable.'

Lena soon got into her stride and started to enjoy herself, and by the end of the exuberant and chaotic first rehearsal, she was exhausted but happy.

'I thought that went well for a first attempt,' she said, as the riders led their horses out of the arena, leaving her and Amos to tidy up. There were a few pieces of paper that had been dropped, and some impromptu props to be put away, but that was about it. 'I think we'll need at least another two goes to get it right,' she added, 'and the final one will have to involve the choir. I thought you did ever so well on the piano.'

Amos pulled a face. 'I haven't played for years. Not since I was a nipper.' He flexed his hands. 'I don't think my fingers will forgive me. Thank goodness one of the teachers will be playing it on the day.'

'You were brilliant,' Lena said. She turned to him, looking him square in the face. 'I really want to thank you for doing this. And Petra, too.'

'Aw, give over. Today was fun.'

'It was, wasn't it?

'Do you fancy coming up to the house for a glass of mulled wine and a slice of Christmas cake before you go?' he asked. 'And I want you to taste a new mulled wine recipe that I've been experimenting with. It's a kid-friendly version, although the adults are welcome to have some, especially if they are driving. I've made it with real blackberries and it's delicious, even if I do say so myself.'

'Ooh, yes please. I could do with warming up before I head off.' Lena rubbed her arms. 'It's a bit chilly in here.'

'I've been thinking about that,' Amos said, threading an arm through hers and leading her outside. 'Mind your step – I didn't realise it was so dark. It'll soon be the longest night.'

Lena shivered. Winter had never been her favourite season, for that very reason. It was only five in the afternoon, and it was already blacker than a witch's hat.

'I've spoken to Dave,' Amos continued, 'and he says that we're welcome to use his patio heaters for the duration. The Black Horse has no need of them at this time of year, and they are only sitting in the shed doing nothing. He suggests switching them on a good couple of hours before the play starts, so the gallery has a chance to warm up before our elderly guests arrive.' He snorted. 'Listen to me! I'm not that much younger than they are.'

'You're years younger!' Lena cried, cuddling into him to avoid the chill wind that was blowing across the yard.

Amos halted and Lena wondered what was wrong. She was keen to get out of the wind and wrap her cold hands around a glass of hot spiced wine. Hopefully, the fire would be lit too, and she could warm the rest of her.

'Hang on a minute,' he said.

They were walking across the yard and had almost reached the house. But instead of hurrying inside, Amos had come to a stop next to a shed door and was reaching inside.

Without warning, the yard was plunged into darkness.

'Oi!' Petra yelled from the depths of one of the stables. 'Switch those lights back on. Some of us can't see a hand in front of our faces!'

'In a minute. I want to show Lena something. Look at that,' he said. His head was tilted back and he was gazing up at the heavens.

Lena looked up and let out a gasp. The sky was inky black and dotted with thousands of stars. She didn't think she'd ever seen so many. And, as she watched, a streak of light travelled overhead, blazing briefly before it petered out. Then there was another, and another.

'It's the Geminid meteor shower,' Amos said in her ear. 'It appears at around this time every December.'

'It's beautiful,' she whispered.

They stood there, arm in arm, watching the flashes of light for a while longer, Lena forgetting about the cold as wonder swept over her. 'This is so humbling. I feel like a very insignificant speck, compared to the wonders of nature.'

'You're not insignificant to me.'

Something in Amos's tone gave her pause, and when she looked at him, he was no longer staring up at the heavens: he was looking at her, his warm breath wreathed around his head like smoke, and his eyes glittering.

 The intensity of his gaze made her catch her breath, and she swallowed nervously. For some reason she was worried that he might be about to kiss her.

Then she feared that he wouldn't.

Petra's voice shattered the moment. 'Amos! If you've finished stargazing, please can you turn the ruddy lights on!'

'Lena, I...' He shook his head, reached around the door and switched them back on.

Lena blinked, her eyes adjusting to the glare as light flooded the yard, and she wondered what he had wanted to say. Had he been about to kiss her, or had she imagined it?

She shivered with sudden longing, but Amos misconstrued the tremor.

'You're freezing. Let's get you inside,' he said, taking the lead once more and guiding her towards the house.

Lena tottered along on legs that refused to do as they were told, her heart thudding so hard she feared he might hear it.

Mortification gripped her. What a silly thing to think. Of course he hadn't been about to kiss her. And she wouldn't have wanted him to.

But for hours later, long after the taste of the mulled wine had left her lips and long after she had snuggled down on the sofa in her living room, she could still feel his gaze on hers. And she was forced to admit that she did want him to kiss her after all, and if he ever did, she might never want him to stop.

'What was all that about?' Petra asked, when Amos returned to the kitchen after escorting Lena to her car.

'Pardon?'

'Switching the lights off. I was in the middle of unsaddling Parsnip.'

'I wanted Lena to see the meteor shower,' he mumbled.

He had no idea what had possessed him to do such a thing. He could simply have told her about it and suggested that she took a look at the sky later this evening. It wasn't as though it was a you-have-to-watch-it-now-or-miss-it event. She could have seen it when she got home, if she had wanted to. The forecast was for a clear night, so there was no risk of cloud cover obscuring the view, either.

But he had wanted to be there when she did. He vividly recalled the first time he'd set eyes on it, and how magical it had been. Mind you, he'd only been a young lad, and in those days everything had seemed magical.

It was odd though, because he'd not thought about that in years, and it was only by chance that he'd happened to glance up at the sky this evening and had spotted a streak of light shoot across it, and realised what he was looking at. For a silly nonsensical second, he had imagined that Mags was sending him a message, because why else would he have seen a shooting star when the yard lights hid most of the night sky from view?

He'd known he was being daft, but...

And then he'd come a cat's whisker to kissing Lena.

Her face, as he'd captured and held her gaze, had given nothing away, so he had no idea whether she would have welcomed his kiss, or whether she would have given him a clip around the ear.

'Are you feeling okay? Is it your heart?' Petra's head was tilted to the side as she studied him, her expression one of concern. Amory was on her lap, sleepy and replete after a feed.

Actually, it **was** his heart that was the problem, but not in the way his niece imagined. 'I'm fine,' he said. 'Stop fussing. I thought we'd have spaghetti bolognese for supper. There's mince in the fridge that needs using.'

Petra made to get up. 'If you take Amory, I'll cook supper. You could probably do with a rest after all that hard work today.'

'I don't need a rest.'

'Let me make it anyway,' she insisted.

'Why? Do you think I'm getting past it?' he shot back crossly.

'Not at all! Whatever gave you that idea?' Petra appeared to be genuinely hurt, and Amos felt a heel.

She was only trying to look after him, and he was throwing it back in her face. Besides, he'd already had the conversation with himself where he had acknowledged that it might be time for her and Harry to start to get used to him not being around. The idea of turning the old feed shed into a bungalow was still bumbling around in his mind. He wouldn't say anything to Petra, yet though. Not until he was sure it was what he wanted to do. And even if he was sure, there was no guarantee the stables would get planning permission, or whether it was even doable. Maybe he should run the idea past Isaac and Nelly first? Isaac could draw up some rough plans and Nelly could give him a ballpark figure as to how much the building work would cost.

Only when he had all that information, could he decide whether his idea was feasible, and if it wasn't he'd have to have a serious rethink, because he was determined that Petra and Harry would have the farmhouse to themselves, without him cramping their style.

CHAPTER SIX

Ten days later saw Lena clapping as enthusiastically as though this final rehearsal was the real thing. Amos was standing by her side, and he was whooping and clapping too.

The headteacher had done them proud, and her pupils had been practising like mad, she'd told them. They had sung an array of traditional carols, some of which would be sung during the play itself, and some afterwards, as well as more modern upbeat songs.

The cast and choir took a bow, the children's faces glowing, bright smiles stretching from ear to ear. They knew they'd done a good job and they'd had fun, too.

'Bravo!' Lena called, earning herself some odd looks from the children, many of whom had probably never heard the expression before. 'You did brilliantly! I'm so proud of you, and I know Amos and Petra are too, as well as your teachers. Your parents are going to be so thrilled!'

The play was far from perfect – how could it be when there were children and animals involved, and they'd only had a couple of weeks to practice? – but she was so incredibly proud of them all.

Suddenly Lena felt herself being picked up and swung around, and she squealed with surprise and delight. But her squeal soon turned to a gasp when Amos landed a smacker on her lips before putting her down.

'Oh!' she cried, her fingers creeping towards her mouth.

Amos immediately looked contrite and took a step backwards. 'I'm sorry, I shouldn't have.'

'I don't mind,' she replied honestly. She hadn't minded one little bit. She had simply been taken aback because she'd not been expecting it. The kiss had been far too fleeting, and she abruptly hoped he would kiss her again. Properly, this time.

'Yes, well...' He was sheepish and uncomfortable, and Lena wondered whether he wished he hadn't done it, in case it gave her the wrong idea about their relationship.

Cheeks flaming, she turned to the cast again, who were milling around, preparing to leave, and she tried to put the kiss to the back of her mind. There would be time enough to mull it over later, when she was alone.

She tilted her head to Amos and hissed out of the side of her mouth, 'We must get the children a little something from Father Christmas.' She raised her eyebrows meaningfully, hoping he would understand what she was getting at.

Amos gave her a sideways look. 'Oh, no, not this year!'

'You **mus**t! You're the most perfect Santa Claus ever!'

'Because I'm old, plump and whiskery? You know how to flatter a fellow.'

'Because you're kind and you've got the most adorable crinkly eyes,' she countered. There was no way Amos could be described as plump (far from it), and he wasn't old, either. Not as far as she was concerned. 'Maybe you are a little on the whiskery side,' she conceded, 'but that's because you have a beard.'

He scratched his chin, and Lena's eyes were drawn to it. She had never kissed a man with a beard before, and although the contact just now had been fleeting, it hadn't been as scratchy as she might have thought.

She stamped down on the urge to kiss him.

'Do you really think I should dress up as Father Christmas again this year?' he asked, frowning.

'I do. The children will love it, and so will the oldies. Take my mum, for instance: she adores getting a present from Santa, even though she knows it's you under the costume.'

'She does? Drat! I didn't think anyone had realised.'

Lena was about to tell him that his disguise wasn't that good, when she realised he was teasing her.

'I'll do it,' he agreed, 'but on one condition. You have to dress up as an elf.'

Lena snorted. 'I'd make a terrible elf!'

'I think you'll make an adorable one.'
Amos was gazing at her with an
unreadable expression on his face.

Did he mean what he'd just said, or was
he just being nice?

She caught her bottom lip between her
teeth and worried at it for a moment
before saying, 'I've not got an elf costume
and it's a bit late to buy one. The play is
only two days away, and there's still so
much to do.'

'You're not getting out of it that easily,'
he warned. 'I'm sure that between us we
can cobble something together.'

'If I'm going to do this, I want a proper
elf outfit, not a cobbled together one,' she
replied haughtily, hoping that was the
end of the matter.

Two of the teachers were still in the arena, waiting for parents to pick up their children, and Lena was mortified when Amos called to then, 'Have either of you got an elf outfit that Lena could wear?'

'I have,' one of them said. 'We'll be wearing our Christmas jumpers, so she can borrow mine. It's a bit short but it does have lovely thick stripey tights to go with it, and I bought a red cape with a white fluffy trim in case I got cold. You're welcome to borrow that, too.'

'Great,' Lena muttered under her breath. 'I can't wait.'

'Thanks,' Amos replied, then looped his arm through Lena's. 'I think me and you have some gift buying to do. If you've not got anything planned, how about we meet in Picklewick in the morning? I'll treat you to a coffee in the cafe before we start. And if necessary, we'll have a spot of lunch out, too.'

Lena readily agreed, despite knowing it wasn't wise to get too used to Amos's company, and she was already looking forward to spending the biggest part of the day with him tomorrow. Resolutely she pushed the uncomfortable worry away that once this play was done and dusted, she was going to miss him far more than was good for her.

'I'm going to have a slice of pumpkin spiced cake and a butterscotch latte to go with it,' Lena announced. She was examining the selection of festive cakes and drinks on offer in the cafe, while Amos contented himself with examining **her**.

He couldn't help marvelling at how lovely she was, especially when she smiled. And right now she was smiling a lot. He loved her pert nose, her generous mouth and her expressive eyes, and he was pleased to see that the sadness which usually lurked in their depths wasn't there today.

She looked cute – if he was allowed to call her that, considering neither of them were spring chickens. Bundled up in a brightly knitted hat, a matching scarf and thick woollen coat, she was also wearing tan-coloured boots with a cream faux fur trim, and she looked very festive and wintery.

'I'll have the same,' he said. 'Why don't you grab a table and I'll place our order?'

By the time he joined her on the squashy sofa next to the window, she had removed her hat, scarf and coat, to reveal a knitted cream dress, and he thought she looked incredibly elegant. It made him feel rather scruffy by comparison, with his brown cord trousers and a sweater that he'd had for years. At least he was wearing a flannel shirt underneath it, in a matching colour, so he didn't look a total mess. He wished he'd made a bit more of an effort though, and he told himself to up his game— before realising there was little point. After the way she had reacted when he'd inadvertently kissed her yesterday, it was clear that Lena didn't consider him to be anything other than a friend.

If he was honest, he hadn't expected her to. Lena was so much younger than he, and had so much more going for her. She could have her pick of any number of men, so why would she be interested in an old codger like him?

'You're looking smart,' she said, and it took Amos a second to realise that she wasn't being sarcastic.

'This old thing?' He gestured to his sweater with a wry grin. 'I've had it for years.'

'The colour suits you.'

It was a shade Petra referred to as heather, and the plaid shirt was a mix of deeper and lighter purple check, with cream. She'd bought both the jumper and the shirt for him a few Christmases ago, and he thought they were past their best now. A bit like him.

'And you look...' he began, coming to halt when he couldn't find the word he wanted, settling for, 'Beautiful.' She was so much more than that though...

Lena's eyebrows shot up. 'Thank you,' was all she said, but she looked pleased, if a little surprised.

'What do you think we should get for the children?' Amos asked, as the waitress placed their drinks and cake on the table. He looked up at the woman and smiled. 'Thanks, this looks delicious.' Picking up a fork he dug in.

'It's going to be difficult, as their ages differ so widely,' Lena pointed out, popping some cake into her mouth and closing her eyes. 'Gosh, this is wonderful!' she exclaimed.

It was, but Amos was more enthralled by the blissful expression on her face, rather than with the cake he was eating. When she opened her eyes again, they were shining with delight.

'I could get used to this,' she said. 'We ought to make it a regular thing.' Then she blushed. 'I mean, if you want to. You don't have to. I expect you've got enough to be going on with without keeping me company on a regular basis.'

'I agree, we **should** do this again. And I don't have anything else to do, but even if I did, I like keeping you company.' Amos put his fork down and took a steadying breath. He might as well tell her once and for all, so he knew where he stood. 'I like **you**.' There, he'd said it.

Lena's expression didn't give anything away as she replied, 'I like you, too.'

'I mean—' he began, anxious that she didn't think he was just being friendly or polite.

'I know what you mean,' she interrupted, and a slow smile spread across her face.

'Oh, my. Well, that's...er...' Amos stuttered to a halt, his heart thumping.

They were interrupted by Charity calling, 'Hiya, you two! I thought yesterday went really well.' She was making her way towards them. 'I'm off to work, but I thought I'd pop in for a sandwich to take with me. We don't seem to have anything in the fridge.'

'It was good, wasn't it?' Lena beamed. 'Amos and I are going to buy a few gifts for Santa to give out after we finish this.'

'What a lovely idea,' Charity said, then eyed the cake, which had hardly been touched. 'That looks yummy.'

'It is.' Lena pulled a face. 'I wonder if you have any ideas of what we can get for the children? There's quite a range of ages and we're a bit stumped. And if you've got any thoughts on what we could buy for the Honeymead residents, that would be a great help, too.'

'You don't want much!' Charity laughed. 'Let me see...' She tapped her fingers against her chin as she thought.

Amos took a sip of his coffee, thankful for the respite. He had been floundering a bit, after Lena had told him she liked him too, wondering if she meant what he hoped she meant or... Bugger! All this thinking was making his head hurt. He was too old for this nonsense. At his age he should be able to tell someone how he felt about them without all this palaver.

But the problem was, the last time he had told a girl he liked her, was forty-odd years ago and he'd ended up marrying her!

Lena was itching to tell her mum about the play – it was such a big part of her life at the moment and was consuming her every waking minute right now – but she didn't want to spoil the surprise, so when she called into the care home after the shopping trip with Amos, she kept her lips zipped firmly shut.

'Hi, Mum, sorry I'm late, I did a bit of Christmas shopping.' She gave the wrinkled cheek a gentle peck, then sat beside the old lady.

Her mum was lying on her bed, pillows propping up her frail body, and Lena felt the prick of tears behind her eyes when she saw her. Olive looked even more fragile today, if that was possible. Her skin had a sallow tinge to it that Lena didn't like, and her hair seemed even wispier than it had yesterday. Even fully dressed, she was worryingly thin and she didn't look as though she had a scrap of fat on her.

Her mum was fading before her eyes, and there wasn't a damn thing Lena could do about it.

With false bonhomie, she said, 'Why aren't you in the day room with the others? That programme you like is on: you know, the one where you have to guess the answers to cryptic clues.'

Olive shrugged, a tiny movement. 'Don't feel like it.'

'Shall I put the tv on in here, and we can watch it together?'

'Don't bother. I'm not interested.' Her voice was weak and croaky, as though she was struggling to find the energy to speak.

Lena bit her lip. Tears were perilously close to the surface, but she didn't want to break down in front of her mum. There would be time enough for crying later, when...

She coughed to cover the lump in her throat and the pain in her heart, shoving the awful thought to the back of her mind and resolving to try to be cheerful for her mum's sake.

Gently she placed her hand over her mother's limp one, curling her fingers around it. She wanted to squeeze her tight and never let go, but she contented herself with holding her hand, conscious of how it resembled a baby bird with the veins and the bones clearly showing through the stretched-tight skin.

'What's going on?' Olive asked, her voice suddenly stronger. 'I know something is up with you. I can tell.'

There was so much, that Lena didn't know where to start. First and foremost was the knowledge that her mother wasn't long for this world. But she suspected her mum already knew that. Secondly, there was the problem of her loneliness, which would only get worse when her mum passed. Then there was Amos, and the growing feelings she had for him. She hoped he was starting to feel the same way about her, but short of asking him, she couldn't be certain.

'Are you happy, Lena?'

'Eh?' Lena snapped to attention. Her mum sounded like the woman she used to be, strong, determined and capable, and a worm of hope burrowed its way into Lena's heart. Perhaps Olive wasn't as frail as she'd thought?

Something in Lena's face must have given her away because her mum continued, 'I didn't think so. And don't go blaming it on me being in here and not having long to live.' Olive shot her a look, her stare fierce. 'I know I'm dying and so do you, so don't pussyfoot around it.' She held Lena's gaze. 'As I was saying, you haven't been happy for a long time. Not since you retired. You need something to keep you occupied, my girl – and I don't mean looking after an old biddy like me.'

Lena was dumbstruck. This was the most animated she'd seen her mum in a long time. Trust it to be because she was telling her off. Even at this stage in her life, Olive wasn't backwards in coming forwards where putting Lena straight was concerned.

'What do you suggest, Mum?' she asked, thinking that Olive was more perceptive than she gave her credit for. Her mum was also right – Lena **wasn't** happy.

She had moved to Picklewick to live with her, when it became clear that the old lady wasn't managing on her own. At this point Lena had been able to carry on working, mostly remotely with the occasional visit to the office for meetings and to catch up. She'd had a responsible job and had loved it. But a couple of years later, when the company had gone through a restructure and early retirement with a substantial redundancy package had been on offer, Lena had taken it. By this time her mum had needed quite a lot of help, and juggling caring for her mother whilst having such a demanding job was becoming increasingly difficult.

'That's for you to figure out,' Olive said. 'All I know is, that you've gone from being busy all the time, to doing next to nothing apart from visiting me. It's not healthy.' She sent Lena a sideways look. 'Maybe you should think about getting yourself a man?'

Lena gasped. 'What on earth makes you say that? You know I haven't bothered with men much since October was born.'

'Perhaps if you had, you wouldn't be so flaming miserable now. You need someone to share your life with.'

'**You** didn't,' Lena retorted. 'After Dad died, I didn't see you whooping it up with anyone.'

Olive pursed her lips. 'That's where you're wrong,' she said. 'I had my moments. It didn't stop me from grieving for your father, but if I had been lucky enough to find a man I wanted to be with for the remainder of my life, I wouldn't have hesitated.'

'That's just it,' Lena said. 'I've never found the right man. I thought October's father might have been, but it wasn't to be. And I can't say I've missed not being married.'

'Are you working on the premise that you can't miss what you've never had?' Olive asked.

'Not at all. I'm working on the premise that, like you, I haven't found anyone I want to be with.' Unfortunately, a blush began to creep up her neck and into her face, giving lie to her words.

'I still think there's something you're not telling me,' Olive persisted. 'And I reckon it's to do with a man.'

'What on earth gives you that idea?'

'I've seen the way you look at him.'

'Look at **who**?'

'Amos Kelly.'

Lena spluttered. 'I don't know what you mean.'

'I think you do, my girl. And for your information, he looks at you the same way.'

'You're going doolally.'

'My body might be falling apart but my mind isn't,' Olive shot back. 'I've got eyes in my head.'

'We're just friends,' Lena insisted. 'Anyway, even if I did think of him in that way, I'm not sure the feeling is reciprocated. He is still in love with his wife.'

'I expect he is. Just because someone dies, it doesn't mean to say you stop loving them. But it is possible to love more than one person at the same time. If I had met someone after your father died and had fallen in love with him, I would still have loved your father. There would have been room in my heart for both of them. Just as there will be room in Amos's.'

Lena was lost for words, conflicting emotions surging through her. Should she admit to her mum how she felt about Amos? Although she wasn't entirely sure how she **did** feel. She knew she liked him immensely, and found him incredibly attractive. She loved spending time with him, and she was hopeful that their friendship would carry on beyond Christmas. But none of these things, even added together, meant that she was contemplating having a serious relationship with him.

'Okay,' she conceded. 'I like Amos a lot. And I think he might like me. But aren't we a bit old for all that?'

Her mother snorted. 'Don't be daft. You're never too old for love.' She drew in a shuddering breath, and seemed to sink back into her pillows. 'Anyway, I've said my piece. I'm tired now. I think I need to sleep.' Her eyelids drifted shut, and within seconds she was deep in slumber.

Lena sat with her for a while, watching the shallow breaths rising and falling in her mother's skinny chest, and she thought about what she had said, that maybe it wasn't too late, either for her or for Amos. Lena just needed some courage, and some indication that Amos was of the same mind. The last thing she wanted was to make a fool of herself. She valued his friendship too much for that. He'd said earlier today in the cafe that he liked her, but they'd been interrupted before she could explore what he meant, and then the conversation had moved on and it had been too late to revisit it.

She thought about how nice today had been. They'd almost been like a proper couple, trundling around the little shops in Picklewick, picking out gifts for the residents of Honeymead, working on the suggestions that Charity had given them. It had been fun, and they had chatted and laughed non-stop right the way through the leisurely lunch which had followed.

She had been tempted to invite him back to her house for supper, but decided that he probably had things to do. And she had wanted to pop in and see her mum, so she'd let it go.

Now, though, she wished she hadn't, because if Amos had joined her for supper, she might have found the courage to ask him if he could ever think of her as more than just a friend. After all, what did she have to lose? If she scared him off, they could simply go back to the way they had been before. And since there was a very strong likelihood that her mum wouldn't need the services of the care home for a great deal longer, Lena wouldn't be visiting Honeymead much, and therefore wouldn't bump into Amos.

However, the thought of not having him in her life hurt her more than she thought possible, and she wrung her hands in worry.

She'd not mention anything, she decided. It simply wasn't worth the risk of losing his friendship. She would have to find something else with which to fill her time and her thoughts, once Christmas was out of the way.

But the problem was, how was she going to fill the hole in her heart — the Amos-shaped hole which she hadn't been aware was there until she'd felt his lips briefly

brush against her mouth and his soul
brush against hers.

CHAPTER SEVEN

It was one of the acknowledged truths that old age doesn't come by itself, and tonight it had brought insomnia with it to keep it company. Which was why Amos was slumped in an armchair in the snug at stupid o'clock in the early hours of the morning on the day of the nativity play, contemplating his navel in front of the dying embers of the fire.

He stirred briefly at the blarting sound of his great-great-nephew demanding a feed, but soon settled down again when he heard the creak of the floorboards on the landing telling him that Petra had gone to see to her son. He wished he could have fed the baby a bottle to give Petra an uninterrupted night's sleep, but Amory was still being breastfed and she hadn't expressed any milk.

Hark at him, knowing about expressing milk and breastfeeding! Who'd have thought it! He smiled wryly to himself, thinking that this time two years ago, it had been just him and Petra at the stables, with no hint on the horizon of the changes that were about to sweep through both their lives. And he had an unsettling feeling that those changes weren't done with them yet. Him, especially.

One of them would be of his own making, because he was determined to hand the stables over to Petra soon, and not just in principle. He was going to sign the whole caboodle over to her, lock, stock and barrel of oats. It would then be her business, to do with as she pleased, and considering it would be hers when he died, she may as well have it now. Heck, she and Harry were more or less running it by themselves anyway. All he'd ask is that—

'What are you doing up?' Petra leaned against the door jamb and rubbed her eyes sleepily. 'Do you know what time it is?'

'Two, three...?' He hazarded a guess. 'I couldn't sleep.'

She yawned and padded over to him. He noticed she was wearing socks with cat paws on them, and he thought how young she looked in the soft light of the fire.

'Are you feeling alright?' Her concern was touching.

'Never better,' he said. In a way, he wasn't lying. He did feel good – not physically, because seventy-three came with its own set of aches and pains – but emotionally. Now that he had decided to relinquish his hold on the stables, it was as though a weight had been lifted from his shoulders and he realised it would do him good to make a fresh start in a place of his own.

Petra plopped down into the chair opposite and sighed loudly, stretching her toes out to the fire and wiggling them.

'There's no need to keep me company,' he said. 'Why don't you go back to bed?'

'I'm wide awake, thanks to Amory. He didn't want a feed: the little monster wanted to play. I've put him back down, but no doubt he'll start squawking again in a minute.'

'If he does, I'll bring him down here with me. There's no point in both of us being up, and you need your sleep more than I do.'

'Thanks for the offer, but as I said, I'm wide awake.' She smiled and said softly. 'What would I do without you?'

He nodded sagely. 'You'll manage. Er, I've been thinking...'

'Uh oh!' She looked worried.

'It's nothing bad,' he assured her hastily.

'Go on.' Her eyes narrowed, glittering in the flickering light from the flames.

'I'm going to sign the stables over to you after Christmas. You'll own it outright. It's about time.'

'**What?** No! The stable is yours. It belongs to you.'

It's more yours and Harry's than mine, these days. And it'll simplify things when the time comes.'

'The time–? **Oh...**' Her face fell when she realised what he meant. 'Don't say that.'

'It happens to all of us sooner or later, although I am hoping it will be later. Don't worry, I'm not ill or anything. Just feeling my age, that's all. I should have retired years ago. I'm as much use as a ladder to a fish.'

She gave him a keen look. 'Is that what you think? Just because you don't do the yard work, doesn't mean to say you don't do your fair share. You do loads: the bookings, the accounts, all the ordering, you run the house, you do the shopping, your look after Amory—' She stopped, and her eyes widened. 'Are you saying you don't want to do it anymore?'

'Not in so many words. I'll still help, but you need your own space. And there's something else – I'll be moving out.'

Petra's mouth dropped open and she stared at him, stunned. 'Where will you go?'

'Not far. I was thinking that turning the feed shed into a bungalow might be a good idea. I'll still be on site, but I won't be in your hair. This—' he gestured to the room at large '—will become **your** home. Yours, Harry's and Amory's. Not mine. I'll have my own behind the yard, so I won't have gone far, and I'll be close enough if you need me.'

'A **bungalow**?' Her eyes were wide, all traces of sleepiness having gone.

'Don't you think a bungalow is a good idea?' Amos began to worry. 'I thought it would be better for me, now that I'm getting older. I don't know how long I'll be able to manage those stairs. I mean, I'm fine now, but what about in the future?'

'A bungalow isn't the problem,' she replied shortly. 'That you are thinking of moving out of the farmhouse, is. This is your home, Amos. I can't drive you out of it.'

'**You're** not driving me anywhere. I **want** to go.' He studied her face carefully, and was dismayed to see her eyes fill with tears.

Before she could say anything, Amos leapt in. 'Don't go getting the wrong end of the stick. I want a place of **my** own because you need a place of **your** own. And, as I said, I've got to think about those damned stairs. And the bath. I can barely get in and out of it as it is.'

'We can have a stairlift put in, and what about one of those walk-in baths?'

'And what if you have more children? They'll need their own bedroom, and the farmhouse only has three.'

'We can convert the attic.'

'It's easier to have a purpose-built bungalow,' he countered.

'You're serious, aren't you?'

Amos pursed his lips and nodded. 'I am.'

'Is there anything I can do to make you change your mind?'

He barked out a laugh. 'Anyone would think I'm emigrating to Spain or going on a world cruise for six months. I'll only be just across the way.'

'Is this why you've been out of sorts recently? Although I've noticed that you have perked up since you came up with the nativity play idea.'

Wincing because she'd noticed and he hadn't been as good at hiding it as he had thought, he said, 'Partly,' then paused, before confessing, 'I was beginning to feel useless, old, past it; but as you pointed out, I've been happier since we started planning the play.'

'What will happen once Christmas is over?'

He blinked at her shrewdness. 'I'm hoping I might have something else to keep me occupied.'

'Lena?' she guessed.

He shrugged. 'I haven't yet plucked up the courage to tell her how I feel, and I'm still not convinced she thinks of me as anything other than a friend, so I'm not getting my hopes up too much.'

'It'll work out,' Petra said. 'And although I don't want you to move out of the house, I can appreciate your reasons. Thank you for trusting me with the stables. I know how much it means to you.'

'It means as much to you too, and I know I'll be leaving it in safe hands.'

Tears trickled down her cheeks and she sniffed loudly. 'I love you, Amos. I just want you to be happy.'

'I love you too, precious girl.' His own eyes brimmed with unshed tears as he watched her leave the room.

Lena wanted to squeal with excitement when she peeped into the arena and saw the old folks being escorted to their seats. She felt like a stage director, hiding behind the curtain before it went up, as she watched the auditorium fill up as the punters filed in, and she hugged herself with excitement.

Piano music filled the air, played by one of the teachers from Picklewick Primary, not quite drowning out the murmur of voices, the shuffling of chairs and the scuffling of feet. Amos and Megan were helping William, Charity and Rose to seat the residents, and they were also handing out plastic glasses of mulled wine to keep them warm and to get them in the mood for the singing they would be expected to do later.

The cast was in the barn, having the final touches put to their costumes, some of which had been kindly leant to the stables from the school's dressing up box, and others provided by parents.

Lena caught sight of Olive, and her heart went out to her. Despite the smile on the old lady's face and the pinkness of her cheeks, her mum looked drawn and tired, and incredibly frail. Her eyes were more alert than they had been for a long time, though, which gave Lena some comfort. Olive was clearly enjoying this unexpected treat, and Lena marvelled at how everyone had managed to keep it a secret from her.

Parents and grandparents were beginning to file in, sitting on the plastic seats behind the far more comfortable ones that the care home residents were enjoying, and the level of noise steadily grew.

'Are we ready yet?' Petra asked, sidling up to her and peering around the door. 'Aw, doesn't it look lovely? You and Amos have worked wonders.'

'Not just us,' Lena pointed out. 'You and Harry have done loads, and so have Nathan and Megan.'

Nathan had found a number of large wooden partitions that had been removed from the cow shed when it had been renovated, and had sanded them down and given them a lick of paint, before joining them together to form a backdrop to the manger scene. The manger itself had been loaned to them by the primary school, as well as some other props such as three little painted chests which represented the gold, frankincense and myrrh, and various bits and pieces from the school's dressing-up box. Nathan had also strung together another couple of panels, which he and Harry had painted to look like a brick wall, and they had found an old door for the innkeeper to stand in front of. Megan had painted a sign that said 'Muddypuddle Inn', which hung above the door, and another smaller one saying 'No Vacancies' was nailed to the side of it.

Petra was providing the donkey, the goats (in lieu of sheep) and a pony dressed in an old sheet which had been painted with black and white splodges to resemble a cow and who sported a pair of fabric horns on its head.

Nathan had also rigged up some lighting, and the whole area was awash with coloured fairy lights as well as a large twinkly star that dangled above the manger scene.

With the carols playing in the background, the aroma of mulled wine and hot chocolate in the air, and the huge Christmas tree in a giant pot that dominated one corner of the arena, the place couldn't be any more festive.

Lena was thrilled with the result, and from their expressions, the people in the audience appeared to be too.

She caught Amos's eye, and he tapped his watch then held up his hand. Lena nodded to indicate that she understood the play was to start in five minutes. Most of the chairs were occupied and she didn't want people to begin getting restless, so five minutes was a good shout.

Lena tugged at the skirt of the borrowed elf costume, praying that it wasn't riding up and showing her stripey backside, and said to Petra, 'Can you ask October and Nathan to start lining everyone up in the correct order? I'll wait here to double-check before they come in. Don't forget, we start with the headteacher and the choir first, then as soon as they are in place, the narrator will come in.'

Lena had had the brilliant idea of letting the narrator, a boy by the name of Billy, do all the talking – from announcing the start of the play right through to thanking everyone for coming. It meant that she didn't have to!

Petra had just taken a step towards the barn where all the participants were waiting, when Lena heard her mutter, 'Bloody hell, I don't believe it,' and she felt her heart constrict with worry as she wondered what was wrong.

Petra chuckled. 'There's Walter from Lilac Tree Farm, and he's only got a bloody sheep with him!'

'You can't have a nativity play without a sheep,' the old man said as he came closer, and Lena saw that the woolly creature was on a lead, and he was carrying a proper shepherd's crook. 'This is Flossie. She's one of this year's lambs. I hand-reared her myself, so she's as tame as that there dog.' He pointed the crook at Queenie. The spaniel was standing at Petra's heel and her ears had pricked up when she saw the sheep.

'Nice to see you, Walter,' Petra said, taking the lead from him. 'How are you?'

'Can't complain,' he said. 'Here.' He shoved the crook at her. 'Give that to one of the shepherds.'

'Thank you, that's very kind. Go and take a seat. I'll look after Flossie.' As soon as he was out of earshot, Petra hissed out of the corner of her mouth, 'We are honoured, indeed. Walter hardly ever ventures far from his farm these days, although he did come to the wedding.'

'I remember seeing him,' Lena said. 'Bless him, he doesn't look at all well. I wonder if he will be the next resident at Honeymead,' she added thoughtfully.

'I doubt it. He'll only leave that farm of his when he's in a box. Right, I'll round everyone up. Break a leg,' she called over her shoulder.

Lena waited for the old man to make his way into the gallery and sit down, then she took a deep breath. This was it!

Time to get this show on the road.

As soon as Nathan dimmed the lights in the arena and the headteacher, followed by three members of her staff and the choir of twenty-three children began to take their places, Amos left the gallery in Charity's capable hands and dashed off to the farmhouse to change into his Santa suit.

Praying that it was going well, he hauled the baggy red trousers up over his legs, and stuffed his feet into his black Wellington boots, before shrugging on the oversized jacket and doing it up. Even from here, the strains of **The First Noel** could be heard, and he found himself humming along to the tune, nerves making his hands shake as he hooked the false beard over his ears and donned the jaunty hat.

With a final check in the mirror to make sure he was presentable, he popped a pair of small round spectacles on the end of his nose and hurried back to the arena. He would watch the performance from the office, not wanting either the children or the old folks to spot him until it was time for his appearance.

He was just in time to hear the choir break into **O Little Town of Bethlehem** and see Jospeh lead Mary, who was perched self-consciously on the bemused donkey, towards the inn.

There wasn't a sound made by the audience as the innkeeper told the couple they could bed down in his stable, and even Amos held his breath at the magic of the scene as Mary and Joseph made their way to the makeshift manger, accompanied by the choir belting out **Away in a Manger.**

Three carols, five shepherds, two goats, one sheep (where did that come from, Amos wondered), three wise men riding on the smallest ponies, and an angel later, and the play was drawing to a close to the haunting music and lyrics of **Silent Night**.

Then as the actors took a bow, the audience burst into rapturous applause, scaring the sheep and the goats, who bleated in alarm, although the horses did little more than flick their ears.

The narrator, who had done a brilliant job, waited for the noise to die down before calling for order. Or rather, he shouted 'Oi! Quiet!' to everyone's amusement.

Petra, October and Nathan hurried into the arena to remove the animals, and as they did so, the choir began to sing **Jingle Bells**, the headteacher encouraging the audience to join in.

This was Amos's cue to get into character.

Hoisting a sack of presents over his shoulder with a grunt, he emerged from the office, crying, 'Ho, ho, ho,' and the audience swivelled in their seats to watch him trundle towards the front of the gallery.

Charity and William stepped forward to help distribute the presents to the care home residents while Amos called out their names, then it was the children's turn. He and Lena had decided on book vouchers as suitable gifts for the kids, and he hoped the children would have fun choosing one. The local bookshop had been very grateful for the custom, and would no doubt welcome this generation of readers with open arms.

'Ladies, gentlemen, and kiddiewinks!' Amos cried, once all the presents had been given out. 'Don't go just yet – we have still got the raffle and we've also got mulled wine, mince pies, hot chocolate, Christmas cake and gingerbread men for those who want it.'

It was no surprise to find that most people did and for the next half hour Amos was kept so busy making drinks and handing out delicious goodies, that he didn't have time to partake of anything himself.

Finally though, the audience began to disperse, taking their children with them, and soon it was time to load Honeymead's residents back onto the bus.

'Ooh, I've had a marvellous time!' one old lady crowed, as William manoeuvred her wheelchair across the yard. She was clutching an empty plastic beaker in her hand, and when she caught Amos's eye, she called, 'Is there any more of this wine? It's gone straight to my head!'

Before he could answer, Amos felt a tap on his arm and he turned to see Lena. She was looking flushed, her eyes were sparkling, and he thought she'd never looked so lovely.

'Can you fetch Gerald for me, and maybe ask October if she could bring Princess and one of the bigger horses?' she asked.

'For your mum?'

She nodded.

'Of course. Give me two minutes.' He scurried off, and was back in less than five, tugging Gerald along behind him.

'I had to bribe him with half an apple,' he said when he reached her. 'I thought your mum might like to feed him the other

half. Shall we go inside? It'll be warmer
for her in there.'

'You are a sweetheart,' Lena said, giving
his arm a squeeze. 'This will mean so
much to her.'

October approached, leading Princess,
who was trying to eat the hem of her
thick jacket, and she also had Storm with
her, Chastity's pretty mare.

'Thank you,' Lena said, with a sniffle and
a grateful smile.

Amos didn't think he could cope with
seeing her cry, not right now, so he
chivvied her along with a forceful, 'Ho, ho,
ho,' and indicated that she should go
ahead of him.

Olive was in her wheelchair, a woolly hat
on her head, a big scarf around her neck

and a heavy blanket tucked around her legs. She looked old and shrivelled, and she also looked exhausted.

Amos had been about to suggest that maybe Olive lingering in the cold to stroke a furry nose or two wasn't the best idea, but he quickly changed his mind when he caught sight of her expression. Her eyes were gleaming and there was a determined set to her thin lips, and he guessed that there was little point in trying to persuade her to leave before she had done what she came here to do.

Hesitantly, he inched forward, praying that Gerald wouldn't make any sudden moves. Lena's mother looked as though the slightest thing would injure her irreparably, and he didn't want to be responsible for causing her any harm.

Impatiently, Olive beckoned him closer. 'My arms aren't that long,' she complained, reaching a trembling hand out toward Gerald's whiskery muzzle. 'There's a good boy,' she crooned, rubbing the donkey under the chin.

'I've got some apple if you want to give it to him,' Amos said, passing it to her. 'If you hold your hand like this—' He demonstrated a flat palm.

'I know what to do. I was riding horses before you were born.' And with that Olive expertly fed Gerald his apple.

The donkey took it gently and crunched it up with enthusiasm. Not to be left out, Princess yanked on her lead rope hard enough to reach a discarded paper plate which sat on a nearby chair, and before she could be stopped, she ate it.

'I see what you mean,' Olive chuckled. 'That goat is a menace.'

After she had admired Storm, who snuffled at the old lady and blew gently through her nose, Amos could tell that Olive had finally had enough.

'I'll help you get your mum onto the bus, if you like,' he said to Lena.

'It's okay, William will do it.' She bent down to kiss her mother's cheek. 'I'll see you tomorrow, Mum.'

'I thought you'd forgotten about me wanting to see the horses, or you couldn't be bothered,' Olive said to Lena in a reedy whisper, slumping back into the chair.

She looked absolutely worn out, and Amos was worried. He had an awful feeling that now she had done what she had wanted to, she might allow herself to drift away in the night. It would be a great way to go (who didn't want to die peacefully in their sleep at the ripe old age of ninety-three?) but it would devastate Lena.

'I wanted it to be a surprise,' Lena told her.

Olive chuckled feebly. 'It was that, all right. Thank you, my lovely girl. And thank you too, Amos.'

'It was my pleasure.' Amos meant it. He'd had a whale of a time helping Lena organise the nativity play, and he was filled with a warm glow of satisfaction as he thought of how brilliantly the afternoon had gone. Everyone had thoroughly enjoyed themselves and the behaviour of the children and the animals had been exemplary.

Olive speared him with her gaze. 'Look after her when I'm gone,' she said suddenly. 'She'll need someone to love.'

Lena let out a gasp. 'Mum!'

'I'm tired. Take me back to the bus.' Olive closed her eyes.

Lena looked at him helplessly and Amos gave her a small smile.

'I will,' he promised the old lady, but she didn't give any sign that she had heard.

With a shake of her head, Lena got behind the wheelchair and rolled her mother outside. He could tell she was embarrassed, and he felt for her, but he was also elated. Somehow, Olive had seen into his heart and approved. Maybe she had seen into Lena's, too? Her words gave him hope that there might indeed be a future for the pair of them.

He pottered around, clearing up discarded cups and paper plates, whilst Megan packed up what little food remained. Amos was pleased to see that most of it had been eaten, and he had to admit that Megan had put on a lovely spread.

'Sorry about my mum,' Lena said, coming back to the gallery and picking up an empty cup to drop into the rubbish bag he was holding.

'Don't be. I'm not.' He looked at her, capturing her gaze. 'I intend to keep my promise,' he assured her.

'There's no need. I'll be fine. Sometimes I think she's losing the plot.'

'Your mother is as sharp as a tack.'

'She's dying.' Lena sank onto a chair.

'Yes, she is.' Amos didn't think there was any point lying to her. 'But she could have a while left yet.'

Lena turned stricken eyes up to him. 'She doesn't. I'll be surprised if she lasts the month. What will I do when she's gone?'

Then she burst into tears and Amos promptly dropped the bag he was holding, sat down in the chair next to her and gathered her to him. He wrapped his arms around her, stroking the back of her head with one hand as she cried.

Her heartbreak brought tears to his own eyes, and for a moment he was catapulted back to the terrible grief he had felt when his own parents had died.

He knew it wasn't going to be easy for her, but he also knew that it wouldn't destroy her. She would mourn her mother's passing, but the grief would eventually ease, although it would never fade entirely. She would absorb it into herself and hold it close until it became a part of her, a brand on her heart that burnt deep but wouldn't consume her entirely.

Eventually, Lena's sobs became sniffles and she gradually sat up straight and wiped her eyes. 'You must think me such an idiot,' she said. 'Mum is still here and I'm acting as though she's already gone.'

'I don't think you're an idiot at all. I think you're incredibly brave. When Mags was ill, I buried my head in the sand for far too long. I kept thinking that she would pull through, that the latest treatment would be a miracle cure. It was only at the very end, when she had hours left to live, that I believed she was truly going to die. I think my denial made it harder to deal with. You are facing your mum's passing with courage. Yes, it'll hurt, possibly more than anything you've experienced before, but you'll cope. And whenever you need a shoulder to cry on, I'll be here.'

'You're such a kind and lovely man,' Lena sniffed. 'Thank you for making Mum's last Christmas so special. I can tell that she was thrilled.'

'She was, wasn't she? And she wasn't the only one.'

A figure appeared at Amos's elbow and he looked around, expecting to see Petra or Megan. Instead, a stranger was gazing down at them curiously.

'Sorry to interrupt,' the woman said. 'I wanted to introduce myself, and the lady outside said that you were the person I need to speak to. My name is Grace Daley and I'm a reporter with The Picklewick Paper. I've been asked to cover the story. Are you Lena and Amos, by any chance?'

'We are.' Amos spoke for both himself and Lena, as Lena hurried to wipe away the remaining tears.

'I must say, that was a heart-warming performance, and the turn-out was impressive. I love that you thought to involve Honeymead's residents, and I understand that this all came about because your mother is unwell, Lena?'

'She's ninety-three. I wanted to make this Christmas extra special for her.'

'You've certainly done that, and for the others. Have you got time for a quick chat? Our readers are going to love this story. I hope you don't mind, but I took a few photos during the performance.'

Lena swallowed and gave Amos's hand a squeeze. 'See, I told you I'd get the stables some publicity,' she whispered. 'Fire away,' she said to Grace Daley.

The woman sat down. 'Brilliant. Right, let's start at the beginning. How long have you two been married?'

Amos was stunned and for a moment he wasn't able to say a word.

What a wonderful idea, he thought, as the image of him and Lena being husband and wife popped into his head.

What an absolutely wonderful, terrifyingly
lovely idea!

CHAPTER EIGHT

'You're daft, you are.' Petra watched Amos give Queenie a wrapped Christmas present, and laughed as the dog tore into it eagerly.

Not to be left out, Tiddles swiped her present with a sheathed paw, then sniffed it suspiciously. The cat didn't look impressed.

They were in the kitchen, and the cat and the dog had been curled up together in Queenie's basket until Amos had enticed them out with a little gift each.

'I've always given the animals presents on Christmas morning. Why should this year be any different?' Amos wrinkled his nose at the baby in her arms, and Amory giggled. 'It's not just good little boys and girls who get presents from Santa,' he said. 'His little face when he saw what was under the tree, was a picture.'

'I'm not sure he knows what's going on. His eyes have been like saucers all morning.'

'You wait until next year. He'll be toddling by then and into everything.'

'Will you still come to the house to see him open his presents?' Petra asked quietly.

'Absolutely! Try keeping me away and see where that gets you. Don't look so worried – there's a long way to go before

I move into the bungalow. I haven't even spoken to Isaac or Nelly yet.'

'If you're serious about this, you'd better get a move on. I've heard that they've got more work than they know what to do with. Mind you, I'm not surprised. With him drawing up the plans and with her guys doing the build, they make a good team.'

'Are you trying to get rid of me?' Amos joked.

'Far from it. We don't want you to move out.'

'Yeah, because then you'll have to cook your own Christmas lunch!'

'Not on your life! We're coming to you. You know I can't cook.'

'Speaking of cooking, I'd better check on the turkey. I don't want to incinerate it.' He peered into the oven, but couldn't see a great deal, so he opened the door, wafting away clouds of steam.

'What time did you put it in?' Petra asked.

'Half past four.'

'Please tell me you went back to bed afterwards,' she pleaded.

'No, but I did manage to have a nap in the chair,' he said. 'I'm going to see Lena later, so I don't want to be too tired.'

'God forbid!' Petra joked. 'You might fall asleep when you're canoodling.'

'We don't canoodle.' Amos stuck his nose in the air.

'Well, it's about time you did.'

'Stop matchmaking.'

'I can't help it. You're perfect for one another.'

Amos narrowed his eyes. Ever since the nativity play, when Petra had caught them sharing a celebratory hug after the reporter had gone, she hadn't stopped teasing him.

'If you're going to hang around the kitchen like a bad smell, you may as well make yourself useful and help me prepare the veg,' he said, knowing that the very thought of peeling potatoes would send her running.

'Er, I've got to um...' she said, sidling out of the door. 'I need to change Amory's nappy.'

He smiled as he heard her footsteps pound up the stairs.

Good. Now that he was finally on his own, he'd give Lena a call.

'Happy Christmas,' he said. 'Can you spare a couple of minutes to chat, or have you got visitors?'

'October and Luca have just left. I'm sitting in the chair, with a cheesy Christmas film on the telly, enjoying a glass of sherry before I go to Honeymead for lunch.'

'It's all right for some,' he grumbled jokingly. 'I've been left to cook the dinner all by myself. I'd love to be waited on.'

'I'll wait on you later,' she offered. 'I thought we could have some nibbles for supper. Unless you want to bring a few slices of turkey with you?'

Amos shuddered. 'Good grief, no! One turkey meal a day is enough. We'll be eating it well into next week as it is.'

He grinned. It was so nice chatting with her, sharing easy banter, and he realised that as lovely as this morning had been, and as wonderful as it would be to share lunch with his family, he couldn't wait to see Lena later. Her house was a far cry from the chaos and the busyness of the stables, but it wasn't just the peace and quiet he was looking forward to. He was eager to spend time with **her.**

That reporter had started him thinking, and once the thought was in his head he hadn't been able to shift it.

He wanted to marry again. He was ready to share his life with someone, and that someone was Lena. At his age he didn't want a romance or a love affair, he wanted a **wife**.

All he hoped was that Lena was ready for a husband, because he fully intended to ask her to marry him – as soon as he plucked up the courage!

Lena reached across the dining table and dabbed at the corner of her mum's mouth with a serviette, noting just how little lunch Olive was eating.

Worriedly, she caught William's eye, and he shook his head gently. He knew as well as she did that Olive was fading fast. It had been a struggle to get her out of bed and dressed this morning, but the old lady had been hell-bent on having her Christmas dinner in the dining room with everyone else.

Lena was determined to be cheerful however, not wanting her misery to infect anyone else. She had to admit that William and his team had done a marvellous job in creating such a festive atmosphere for the residents. It couldn't be easy for the staff to give up their own Christmas lunches and time that could be spent with their own families, in order to make the old folks' Christmas Day a happy and memorable one.

The dining room had a small Christmas tree in one corner, and lively festive tunes could be heard playing in the background. The tables had been decorated nicely, with white tablecloths, pretty centrepieces and crackers, and the first thing everyone had done as soon as they were seated, had been to pull their crackers, tell a few jokes and wear their paper party hats.

Even Olive sported a bright pink number perched on top of her head, her wispy hair poking out from the sides, and she had even managed to smile at some of the corny jokes.

But only halfway through lunch, the old lady's eyes were drooping and she was clearly finding it difficult. If Lena had thought Olive frail before the nativity play, she was doubly-so now.

In the intervening days, her mum had been slipping away fast, and every time Lena's phone rang, her heart lurched uncomfortably with fear. Any day now one of those phone calls would be the one she dreaded.

She continued to try her best to persuade her mum to eat, even cutting up the food for her, but Olive simply wasn't interested, although she did have a few sips of water, so at least she was drinking.

Lena tried to keep the conversation going. 'Luca has booked a surprise holiday for October as her Christmas present. They're flying out to Mauritius tonight for two whole weeks. Isn't that lovely?'

Olive gave a tiny nod. 'Lucky girl.'

'She is, isn't she? He thinks the world of her. I wouldn't be surprised if he asks her to marry him while they're out there. We might have a wedding to go to soon. Won't that be nice?'

Olive's gaze flickered to Lena, then she blinked slowly and looked away. Lena made a face, hearing her mother's unspoken belief that she wouldn't be around to attend any such wedding, and she immediately felt guilty. Maybe making small talk wasn't such a good idea.

As soon as the Christmas pudding had been served, complete with flaming brandy sauce, Olive indicated that she wanted to go to her room, so Lena drained her wine glass and stood up.

'Let me help,' one of the care assistants said, and Lena gratefully accepted. Although Olive weighed barely more than a bag of sugar, it still wasn't easy lifting her out of her chair and onto the bed, even with the hoist, and Lena was terrified of causing her any pain or discomfort.

Safely tucked in, after being changed into her nightclothes as she requested, Olive sank back into the pillows with a deep sigh.

'Can I get you anything, Mum?' Lena asked. 'A nice cup of tea?'

Olive shook her head, a small movement, which clearly cost her some effort. 'I just want to sleep.'

And it was at that moment, Lena realised her mum was ready to go, that she had been ready to go for a while. Lena suspected her mum had been hanging on for Lena's sake, not for her own.

Suddenly she understood how selfish she was in wanting to hang on to her mum for as long as possible, and she collapsed into the armchair next to the bed and took hold of her mother's frail hand.

'I'll sit with you for a while,' she said, not wanting to leave, scared that her mum would slip away the second she was gone.

'Go home,' Olive ordered, her voice barely more than a sigh. 'Amos will be waiting.'

Lena had told her that Amos was calling around this afternoon and they were to have supper together, but now she was having second thoughts. What if she went home, and her mum passed away without her being there? She'd never forgive herself.

As though sensing Lena's thoughts, Olive whispered, 'Come and see me tomorrow.'

'But—'

'But nothing. Go home. I'll still be here tomorrow.'

Lena wanted to say 'promise?', but she didn't want to place that burden on her mum, so she did the only thing she could. She kissed her gently on the forehead, and slipped out of the room.

'I thought you weren't going to bring any turkey,' Lena stated, as she unpacked the goodies that Amos had brought with him.

There was so much food at the stables, that he had been worried they wouldn't get through it all, so he decided to share it with Lena. And of course, some of it had to be turkey. Even if they didn't eat it now, Lena could have some tomorrow. He'd also brought a couple of slices of Christmas cake which Megan had made, half a Yule log, some cheeses and pickles, and a loaf of bread that he'd baked overnight. If nothing else, they could have turkey and pickle sandwiches followed by a slice of cake.

Oh, and he'd brought a bottle of wine and some stubby bottles of ale, as well. He poured himself a glass of the ale, but he didn't intend to drink more than one, because he would be driving home later. He wasn't much of a drinker anyway, although he did enjoy a pint or two in The Black Horse, especially when he was playing darts. However, he knew Lena liked wine, and he didn't know whether she would have bothered to have bought herself any since she was spending Christmas more or less alone.

'How did lunch go?' she asked as she put the food in the fridge. 'I take it you're not ready for anything to eat just yet?'

'Good lord, no! I'm not sure whether I'll eat ever again, if I'm honest. It was lovely, especially since it was Amory's first Christmas. He settled for milk and some pureed carrot and swede.' Amos shuddered. It hadn't looked at all appetising, but the little boy had wolfed it down. He certainly had a healthy appetite.

'Timothy and Charity popped in for a few minutes,' he told her, 'But Timothy was on call, and Charity had to go to work, so they didn't stay long.'

'Yes, I saw her at the care home. She looked very festive. She was wearing a jumper with a Christmas pudding on the front, and had Christmas pudding earrings.' Lena looked sad.

'How was your lunch?' he asked, knowing that it would have been a bitter-sweet occasion for her.

'The food was lovely as usual, and the staff made such an effort, but Mum didn't seem quite with it. In fact, I didn't want to leave her, but she insisted.'

'You can't be with her twenty-four hours a day,' Amos pointed out.

'I know, but it could happen any day now, and I want to be there when it does. I know they'll call me when the end is near, but what if they don't realise?'

'They will,' Amos assured her. 'Someone will check on her every few minutes, you know that.'

Lena nodded uncertainly. 'I know, but...' She trailed off.

'Come here,' Amos said, opening his arms wide. 'I think you need a hug.'

When she stepped into his embrace, he breathed in the scent of her perfume and thought how good it was to hold her. It felt right, as though it was meant to be, and he hugged her closer.

She rested her head against his shoulder and hitched in a deep breath. 'Don't worry, I'm not going to cry,' she said her voice slightly muffled.

'I don't mind if you do,' he said. 'I'm just glad that you feel you can share it with me.'

Lena pulled back a little and looked him in the eye. 'You're an easy man to share things with,' she said.

Then she kissed him.

Amos was shocked and it took him a heartbeat or two to recover, but suddenly he was kissing her back, and he marvelled how soft and warm her lips were, and how excited he was beginning to feel, as a fire that he had thought had long been extinguished, burst into flickering flame in his stomach.

Her fingers dug into his hair, pulling his head down as she kissed him passionately, and he lost himself in the sensations coursing through him, conscious only of her mouth, her hands on his back and her body pressed up against his.

Eager to take it further but aware that perhaps now was not the best time, Amos reluctantly drew away. He still kept hold of her, his arms refusing to let go, as he looked deep into her eyes, seeing his own hunger reflected back at him.

'I've been wanting to do that for a long time,' she said, her voice soft.

'Me, too. But, I was scared of losing your friendship.'

'You're not losing anything, you're gaining something. We both are.'

'Are you sure this is what you want?'

'I've never been surer of anything,' she replied.

He knew that this wasn't a knee-jerk reaction from Lena just because she didn't want to be on her own; and he knew her well enough to understand that she would prefer not to be in a relationship rather than be in one just because she might be lonely.

However, he didn't just want a relationship. Amos wanted a deeper commitment, but the question was, did she?

Lena had never married, so what made him think she would want to marry now?

The only way to find out, would be to ask her. But now wasn't the right time. He would wait until the New Year, until things had settled down and life was back on an even keel, and he would ask her then.

But at this moment there was another question he wanted answering, one that he wasn't afraid of asking. 'Can I kiss you again?'

And his whole being burst into flame when she said. 'You better had!'

Where is this heading, Lena asked herself later that evening, after Amos had left and she was able to breathe.

That first kiss had led to many more; so many that it had been a long time before they'd come up for air. And even when the kissing had stopped and they were eating supper, she still hadn't been able to catch her breath.

Every time she looked at him, (which was often, considering she was unable to take her eyes off him for more than a few seconds at a time) her heart skipped a beat and her tummy churned with excitement. She wanted him to hold her and never let go. She wanted to drag him off to bed and make love with him. Hell, she wanted all of him, body and soul.

But she also wanted to take it slow. Jumping into bed with him after just one kiss (okay, many kisses) wasn't her style. And she had been without a man in her life for so long that she worried she was making a mistake.

Because Lena didn't want a friends-with-benefits relationship.

She wanted long-term commitment. And now that she was alone in the house and had space to think, she realised that this situation was going to be an all-or-nothing one. And that meant marriage.

Finally, after all these years, she was ready for it.

She had found the man she wanted to marry.

But the problem was, would **he** want to marry **her**?

CHAPTER NINE

Sleep had been hard to come by for Lena last night. She had lain awake for hours until Christmas Day faded into Boxing Day, restless and unfulfilled, thoughts swirling and dipping through her mind like a flock of starlings preparing to roost.

Five a.m. saw her awake for good, and she was just about to go downstairs to make a cup of tea, when the phone rang.

She didn't need a crystal ball to tell her who was calling, and dread swept through her. With trembling fingers and clammy palms, she answered it.

Nodding once as she listened to the voice on the other end, all she said was, 'I'll be there in fifteen minutes.'

Slowly replacing the phone on the bedside table, she paused for a moment, not wanting to face the reality of what was about to happen but knowing that she must.

This was it. This was the day she would say goodbye to her mother. This was the day she would be without the woman who had nurtured her and loved her unconditionally all her life.

Steeling herself, Lena quickly threw on some clothes, brushed her teeth and splashed water on her face, and in five minutes she was out of the door and sprinting towards her car.

She remembered nothing of the short drive to the care home as she pulled into the silent car park and cut the engine, praying that she wasn't too late.

The air was still, and daylight was a few hours away yet. Cold seeped through her coat as she got out of the car, but it was nothing compared to the chill that had taken hold of her heart, and she wondered if she would ever feel warm again.

As Lena waited to be buzzed in, platitudes tumbled through her mind: her mother had had a good life, she had lived to a ripe old age, time is a great healer...None of them made a scrap of difference when faced with the reality of her impending loss.

William himself unlocked the door. His expression was sombre and he gestured for her to follow him, even though she knew the way to her mother's room blindfolded.

'Yvonne is with her. She's been with her all night, just in case...' he said.

Lena was grateful that her mother hadn't been left alone.

William added, 'Your mum has been asleep since yesterday lunchtime, but at some point in the night she slipped into unconsciousness.'

'Do you think she's in any pain?'

'No, I don't. She's peaceful.' He halted outside her mother's door, before giving it a gentle tap and pushing it open.

Lena's eyes flew to the bed.

Her mother lay on her back, her body barely more than a slight rise under the bedclothes. She appeared to be asleep, and Lena wondered whether she would rouse enough to realise she was there. She hoped so – she wanted to gaze into her mum's eyes one last time, to know that her voice was the last thing her mum heard in this world as she told her how much she loved her and how deeply she would miss her.

Yvonne was sitting by the side of the bed, holding Olive's hand, and Lena gave the care assistant a tearful smile.

Don't cry, she told herself, **don't cry**. She was desperate for her mum not to see how upset she was, but she couldn't hold back the tears and they spilled over to trickle down her cheeks in a steady stream.

'Thank you,' she whispered, as Yvonne got to her feet.

'I'll be outside if you need anything,' she said, patting Lena's arm as she stepped past her.

'Do you want me to stay, or would you prefer to be alone?' William asked.

'Alone,' she said, her voice breaking. 'Does she know I'm here?'

'I'm sure she does.'

Not taking her eyes off her mum, Lena waited until the door closed softly behind her before walking slowly towards the bed. She had to look carefully to see the almost imperceptible rise and fall of her mum's chest and, as she studied her, she saw how long there was between those shallow, fitful breaths.

She did look peaceful though, and Lena took some comfort from that.

'Mum, it's me, Lena.' She bent over the bed, stroking a strand of hair back from the remarkably unlined forehead, and kissing her gently. 'I love you. I just want you to know that.'

'Lena?' Olive's voice was softer than mist, hardly more than a breath in the warm dimness of the room.

'Yes, Mum, it's Lena.' She straightened up as she realised her tears were falling on the white sheet, and she hastily brushed them away and sat down in the recently-vacated chair.

She took her mother's hand in both of hers and caressed it, letting the stillness of the room seep into her, as memories cascaded through her mind.

She had no idea how much time had passed – it might have been minutes, it might have been hours – when her mother's eyes fluttered open and Lena's gaze snapped to her as Olive uttered a gasp.

'Mum? Can you hear me?' Lena croaked, her voice hoarse.

A faint whisper carried to her ears and she rose stiffly, leaning in so close that she could feel her mother's barely-there breath on her cheek. Tears poured down her face as she struggled to hear what her mum was saying.

Another breath. A last sigh. 'Love you too, Lena. You'll always be my little girl.' Her eyes drifted shut.

There were no more breaths.

Her mother was gone.

Amos shifted uncomfortably in his chair, feeling the stiffness in his hips and knees. A cup of tea sat cold and untouched on the side table next to him and the smell of bacon for the residents' breakfast made him feel nauseous. He couldn't face anything, not even tea, not when Lena's mother was dying in the room down the hall.

'Amos?' Charity hurried towards him. 'William told me about Olive. How's Lena coping?'

He shrugged. Although he would have loved nothing more than to go to her and take her in his arms, he knew she needed this time alone with her mum.

'Not good, I suspect,' he said. 'Olive might have had a good innings, but age is irrelevant when it comes to losing a parent. It still hurts like hell.'

'Lena's lucky to have you,' Charity said, and Amos shot her a keen look.

Did everyone think they were an item?

And was that what they were, after last night?

'What time do you finish today?' he asked, eager to change the subject.

'Oh, I'm not working today. I heard about Olive and I felt I should pop in, what with October being halfway across the Indian Ocean by now. I thought Lena could do with the support.'

Bless her, Charity's eyes were damp and Amos could see she was upset. 'That's kind of you,' he said.

Charity placed her hand over his. 'I'm sure Lena would rather cry on your shoulder than mine.'

'Get off home – I expect Timothy is waiting. I'll tell her you were here. I'm sure she'll be touched.'

'He is.' She smiled for a moment, then she hesitated. 'Are **you** okay?'

It was sweet of her to ask. 'I will be,' he replied, guessing that she realised seeing Lena so upset would bring memories of Mags's death home to him.

She smiled down at him. 'You make a lovely couple.'

'Eh?'

'Olive told me that the two of you are in love.'

'When did she tell you that?' Amos was flabbergasted.

'The day of the nativity play. She said—' Charity gulped, tears brimming '—she said she could die in peace now, knowing that Lena had you to love and cherish her.'

Amos blinked. 'But what if Lena doesn't **want** to be loved and cherished.'

'Don't be silly, Amos! Of course she does! She loves you.'

'**Lena** told you that?'

Charity frowned. 'No, Olive did. Head over heels in love with you, is what she said. Right, I'll be off. I've already been up to the stables this morning, but if you need me, just shout. Look after Lena.'

'I will,' Amos said to her retreating back.

Fancy that! Had Olive really told her that Lena was head over heels in love with him? And if so, how had the old lady known? Had Lena said so? Or was Olive matchmaking?

He was still mulling it over when movement caught his eye, and he saw the forlorn figure of Lena walking slowly down the corridor.

Amos struggled to his feet, cursing his stupidity for sitting still for so long, as he hobbled towards her. He could tell by her face that her mother was gone. She looked pale and incredibly sad, but she brightened momentarily when she saw him.

'I'm so sorry, Lena,' he said, reaching her and pulling her into his arms.

She sank into him, and he felt her tremble as sobs wracked her. There was no need for words and nothing he could say would make her feel any better, so he remained silent and let her cry.

And when her tears eased, he gently wiped her face, and took her home.

'Please stay with me,' Lena pleaded. 'I don't want to be on my own, not today.' She wrapped her arms around her waist and hugged herself. She was freezing, even though the heating was on and the house was warm. It was probably the shock, she thought.

Amos was in the middle of filling the kettle, because what else did one do at a time like this, she mused absently, and as he switched it on, he turned to her.

'I'll stay with you for as long as you want,' he promised.

She would like it to be forever, but... 'Thanks.'

'Sit down, I'll bring the tea in.'

With a deep sigh, Lena wandered into the living room and stared at it with fresh eyes. This was her mother's house – hers now, she supposed – but even though it had been her home since she had returned to Picklewick to live, today it didn't feel like it. Most of the furniture belonged to her mum, and the décor was mostly her mum's taste. Lena hadn't seen the point in changing anything, although she had brought some of her own furniture with her; and a few of October's bits and pieces were also in evidence, although her daughter had taken everything that she had wanted to keep to Luca's house when she'd moved in with him.

'Here you go, a nice cup of tea,' Amos said.

She took it from him and wrapped her hands around the mug without drinking. 'Do you want to know what's strange?' she said. 'Yesterday, if you'd asked, I would have said this is mine, my house, my home, even though Mum still technically owns...**owned**...it. But today, it doesn't feel like mine. From now on, I'll always think of it as **her** house.'

'You're bound to, I suppose. It's full of memories of her. I know I sometimes still see Mags in the farmhouse.'

'No, I don't think that's it...' Lena said. She wasn't entirely sure what she meant, but she knew one thing – she didn't want to live here any longer. 'I want to move,' she said. 'Sell up and buy something smaller. Why do I need four bedrooms? Two will be ample. I want a fresh start.'

'Funny you should say that – I was thinking the very same thing. I'm planning on moving out of the farmhouse and into a bungalow.'

Lena was shocked. 'You are going to leave the stables?' She never would have thought he'd do such a thing.

Amos blew out his cheeks. 'Not exactly. I've told Petra that I want to convert a feed shed into a bungalow. It'll be better for all of us, going forward. Future-proofing, I think it's called. With that in mind, I'm also signing the stables over to her. It'll be hers anyway when I'm gone.' He realised what he'd said, and pulled a face. 'Sorry, that was insensitive.'

'There's no need to tiptoe around me.' Lena took a mouthful of the rapidly cooling tea. 'I think your plan is a sensible one.'

'But maybe you should give yourself time to think about what you want to do? You don't want to make any hasty decisions,' he said.

'I won't do anything yet,' she assured him. There was the funeral and all the legalities to get through first. 'But I'm pretty sure I won't change my mind. Now that you come to mention it, a bungalow sounds perfect.'

Amos was staring at her strangely.

'What?' she asked.

'I'm not sure how to say this, and I know it's the worst timing ever, but... Ah, no, forget it.' He was looking decidedly uncomfortable.

'Spit it out,' she said. 'I won't rest until I know what it is.'

'I wish I hadn't said anything.' He hung his head. 'Me and my big mouth.'

'Amos...?' she warned.

'I was going to suggest that you move to the bungalow with me, but it's the stupidest, most ridiculous idea—'

'Yes.'

His mouth dropped open and his bushy eyebrows shot up to his hairline. He had a good head of hair for a man of his age, she thought absently.

'You will?' He looked stunned.

'I will. But on one condition. I have no intention of being a kept woman or your mistress. I might be old-fashioned and I know that many couples do live happily together without being married, but that's not for me. If I'm going to move in with you, I'll do so as your wife or not at all.' She nearly added 'so there', but instead she pursed her lips, marvelling at how the conversation had progressed so quickly to this point.

Her mum had only just died and here she was, considering selling the family home to move in with a man who hadn't even told her he loved her yet. And – dear god – she had just asked him, in a roundabout way, to marry her.

'You beat me to it,' he said, after a short but very intense silence during which Lena was beginning to think about pleading insanity due to bereavement and buggering off to bed. 'I was going to propose to you, but not for a while,' he added quietly.

'Am I being callous? My mum has only just died and here I am—' She let out a sudden sob, her emotions all over the place.

'No, but if **I** had asked **you** to marry me before you'd had time to come to terms with losing her, then that would be a different thing altogether. I just want to make sure you're not doing anything you regret. I want nothing more than to marry you and I'd call myself the luckiest man in the world if you were my wife, but **love** is what is important here and I love you too much to let you make a mistake.'

He was about to carry on, but Lena didn't let him. 'You love me?'

'I do.'

'Say it.'

'I love you.' He looked nervous and his apprehension touched her deeply.

She put her mug down, took a step closer and said, 'I love you, too. I've loved you for a while. Believe me when I tell you that if we do get married, I won't regret it.' She hitched in a shaky breath. 'It was my mum who made me realise how I felt, and she also made me realise that it's not too late for love. The only thing that was holding me back was Mags.'

Amos's expression clouded. 'Mags? I can understand why, but it's time I let her go. I've clung on to her for far too long, and I know she would have hated that. There's room in my heart for both of you, and although I'll never forget her and I'll always love her, I love you too, and I will for the rest of my life.'

Lena's heart swelled with love, and as she stepped into his waiting arms she thought she heard her mother's voice whisper, 'Be happy, my lovely girl.'

And neither did she think she imagined the gentle stroke of her mother's hand on her shoulder, or the kiss of barely-there lips on the top of her head.

I love you, Mum, she thought, then she was lost in Amos's embrace and the future it held.

This Christmas had been the saddest and the happiest of her life, magical, poignant and wonderful – and with this special man at her side, she found herself looking forward to many, many more.

The Stables on Muddypuddle Lane Series

Spring

Summer

Autumn

Winter

Valentine Kisses

The Patter of Tiny Feet

Wedding Bells

Christmas

About Etti

Etti Summers is the author of wonderfully romantic fiction with happy ever afters guaranteed.

She is also a wife, a mum, a pink gin enthusiast, a veggie grower and a keen reader.

www.ingramcontent.com/pod-product-compliance
Lightning Source LLC
Chambersburg PA
CBHW021244060726
47590CB00005B/1896